SAM CRESCENT AND STACEY ESPINO

EVERNIGHT PUBLISHING ®

www.evernightpublishing.com

Copyright© 2022

Sam Crescent and Stacey Espino

Editor: Audrey Bobak

Cover Artist: Jay Aheer

ISBN: 978-0-3695-0507-1

SAM CRESCENT AND STACEY ESPINO

CLAIMED BY HER COWBOYS

Sam Crescent and Stacey Espino

Copyright © 2021

Chapter One

"There isn't anyone you haven't pushed away or scared off," Archie Wales said.

Gabe Cartwright stood up, tired of being singled out. He wiped the sweat from his brow with his sleeve. There wasn't even a breeze to kill the heat. He looked at his friends and roommates, Archie and Vinny. They had all argued for many weeks about hiring a housekeeper. Personally, he didn't want a fucking stranger walking around their house or anywhere near their shit. He worked hard for everything he had, and he did not trust easily.

"What are you babbling on about now?" He didn't have time for this. There was too much to get done on a working farm without arguing about nonsense. Already, he noticed another fence that required mending, and they had orders that needed to be filled before sundown.

For so long, Archie and Vinny had been after him about hiring a housekeeper. It still hadn't happened.

Most of the people who previously applied were only after easy work. He had yet to hire anyone he could trust.

"Well, we have a winner, thank you very much. The pretty little Annalise has applied, and she also brought tester cookies. Not even you can disagree with this pick." Archie held up a single cookie, and Gabe couldn't argue. They did look tasty, but he wasn't easily swayed by food.

He was the current cook on the ranch, and the boys were used to one thing, steak and potatoes. That was all. He didn't need to learn to cook anything else.

"Come on, man, you have got to try these. They're so good. They're going to give you wet dreams."

"Not happening," he said, bending down to fork the straw from one pile to another. He noticed out of the three of them, he was the only one working. "If you want to get this job done today, and get an early night, hurry up."

Vinny chose that moment to laugh. "Come on, we work our asses off all the time. And you're the one working harder than anyone else—cleaning, cooking. It's work you don't need to do. We can afford to hire, Gabe."

"We've got up to five ranch hands already."

Gabe knew they were well off. After all their hard work, ranching was finally turning a profit, a pretty healthy one, but he wasn't about to tell the guys it was because of a few investments on the stock markets that had kept this place open.

He, Archie, and Vinny had been best friends since they were kids. All of them came from deadbeat families, with drunks or addicts as parents. Gabe got his work ethic from not wanting to end up like his dad, not by example.

Together, they had joined as a unit. Just the three of them, working two and three jobs at a time to help get a down payment for this place. Even as a kid, the Hollington Ranch had been in disrepair. They would sneak off to the ranch for a place to hide while their parents were having one of their benders. Mr. Hollington would leave out snacks and sodas, along with blankets and cushions. He never said anything to them. Never told them off nor called the cops. He was a good guy.

The news of his passing had hit them all hard, and even though they weren't invited to the funeral, they each went and paid their respects. The ranch went up for sale, but no one bought it until they did.

It had taken a lot of years, hard work, and love, but the ranch house was back in impeccable condition. The land once again had cattle, and they had expanded to allow horse boarding, cash crops, as well as renting out small animals for kids' events. They may be simple cowboys, but their entrepreneurial spirit got them where they were.

Ranch life was busy most of the time, and if he was honest with himself, Gabe preferred it that way. Too much time in his head was never a good thing.

A housekeeper would ruin the peace they'd taken years to find. At the same time, steak and potatoes had long lost its appeal. The cookie Archie ate had looked good.

"Let me try one of them," he said.

Archie tossed the bag in his direction, and he caught it, not surprised to see there was only one left.

After taking it out, he took a bite, and fuck him, he'd never tasted anything so good. It was sweet, but not too sweet. Each bite seemed to have just the right amount of chocolate chips in it. There was even a hint of salt that he loved.

"Damn," he said.

"She's a good cook, but she's willing to come in

and cook for us for a full day—breakfast, lunch, and dinner. She'll also work on a trial basis," Archie said.

Gabe finished the cookie in two bites, and the moment he swallowed the last mouthful, he mourned his cookie. This was ridiculous. He was a grown man. He didn't get sad over baked goodies.

"Give me more details."

Vinny coughed, and Gabe glared at him. The fucker never knew how to hide a laugh.

"She's thirty years old. Has really nice red hair, green eyes. Never been married. Isn't in a relationship. She's really sweet and is just looking for a job with housing. Her current apartment has been sold for a renovation, but because of the cost, she can't afford to keep it. She is also the hot, curvy woman who works at the diner three times a week."

"Curvy Red?" Gabe asked.

He rarely went into town, but when he did, he always chose to eat at the diner, and he'd recognized the curvy red waitress at the bar. Who hadn't?

His gaze had been drawn to her uniform, which was a size too small for her lush frame. Damn it.

Every time he was served by Curvy Red, he'd been hard as fucking rock. He didn't want any distractions, but if she failed a trial run, he'd finally get Vinny and Archie off his back, and that was well worth it.

"Call her in."

****

Archie was excited.

They had tried keeping a housekeeper a couple of times, but it had always ended in disaster. One had promised to be a good cook and had given them all food poisoning. Another tried to feed them nothing but vegetables and later told them they didn't know how to cook at all. Then there was the one who had tried to rob from them, and they ended up getting the sheriff involved, and that had been the final straw for Gabe. After that, no more housekeepers, and they'd all lived on a diet of diner food, and steak and potatoes.

He hated steak.

And potatoes.

He also hated watching Curvy Red at the diner, wanting to ask her out but never having the nerve. He was forty years old yet still felt like a skinny, awkward teen when he was around her. Most of his childhood memories were of getting beat up and trampled on as the school runt—until he grew up and began lifting weights. He never seemed to stop growing once he hit his early twenties, and now he was bigger, taller, and stronger than all the boys he'd once grown up with. Still, those fucking insecurities ran deep, and he couldn't muster up the nerve to ask out Curvy Red.

When he saw her application, he'd immediately called her and started to ask questions.

Opening the door to her now, he offered her a smile. She held on to her bag like a lifeline, and he noticed her smile didn't quite reach her eyes. Was he that imposing?

It was strange what he noticed about this sweet woman. She was thirty years old, and from what he could tell, never had a boyfriend. The apartment building where she lived was a piece of shit. He knew as he'd grown up around there. Diapers, used condoms, and even syringes littered the floors. It wasn't a good place to live, but it was cheap. Since she was being evicted, he assumed the building was being knocked down and rebuilt into overpriced condos. It would be no surprise. The town wanted to bring new investments and opportunities to the community, calling it gentrification.

What did surprise him was that Annalise came from a good family. Her mother was a churchgoer, and they lived on a good estate. Her sisters were also quite wealthy, marrying into money.

Annalise was like the black sheep of the family. He didn't get it. But he certainly wasn't going to question her taking a job with them. He felt like he'd won the fucking lottery.

"Hi, I'm early, right? I hope that's okay."

"It's six in the morning. I'm shocked. I expected you at nine."

"Well, I asked a couple of guys that work for you and they said you're always up early to handle jobs on the ranch, and I figured I would work to your schedule." She bent down, and he noticed the brown paper bags.

"What's all this?" he asked.

"I didn't know what kind of food you'd want, and well, I want to make you guys a good breakfast. I got everything I could think of for breakfast, lunch, and dinner."

"You didn't have to do that," he said. He couldn't guarantee Gabe would even give her the job. He was the one who handled all of their finances. Archie still couldn't figure out how they were able to buy this place, refurbish it all, and hire men to help.

The guy was a miracle worker. He was also five years old than him and Vinny.

Archie also had an inkling that Gabe liked Annalise. Whenever they went to eat at the diner, he was always watching her. Her body was quite distracting.

He hoped having someone Gabe was attracted to might sweeten the deal.

The only problem he saw was that he liked Annalise as well, and with his great powers of observation, he would put money on it Vinny had a thing for her as well. Not good. All three of them having a thing for the same woman. Maybe this wasn't such a good idea after all.

"Let me grab those for you." He grabbed the brown paper bags. "I'll show you around, and then you can get started."

They headed straight to the kitchen first. Putting the bags down, he pointed around him. "The kitchen."

She chuckled.

He loved the sound and knew he wanted to make her laugh often.

"Come on. It's a quick tour." He showed her the whole of the downstairs. The living room, dining room, and the small library that was also Gabe's office. He warned her not to touch Gabe's desk at all. Even he got yelled at for touching the man's desk.

With the downstairs done, he told her they would tour the upstairs later. First, she needed to actually pass the cooking test.

Gabe wouldn't like anyone going upstairs, so that was strictly off-limits.

"Is there anything else you need?" he asked.

"Nope. I'm good. I can handle this."

"Okay, great."

"Are you nervous?" Annalise asked.

"Look, I don't want to get your hopes up, but Gabe isn't on board with the whole housekeeper thing. He's the one doing the hiring. I ... I just hope this goes well."

"It's fine. Honestly." She shrugged.

"Why do you want to work for us?" Archie asked.

"I love this place, for one. I remember seeing Mr. Hollington in town. Every Wednesday he'd go to the cemetery. He had family there. He was such a sad man, but whenever he saw me, he'd give me this smile that said everything was going to be okay. When I saw your ad in the paper, I don't know, I felt I had to come and help out where I could. Sounds silly."

"Not at all. I appreciate it."

"And, of course, I need a job and a place to stay, so this would be perfect."

He put a hand on her shoulder and immediately let go. The attraction he felt for this woman was going to have to stay in check. Not once had Annalise ever given him the inkling she wanted anything from him. She was prim and proper to a fault.

Always sweet. Always kind. Always so very thoughtful.

Blowing out a breath, he left her to it and found Vinny in the barn.

"How did it go?" Vinny asked.

"I have no idea. She's in the kitchen now. I hope she doesn't burn it down."

Vinny rested his shovel on the ground, leaning on the handle. "You're really nervous about all of this."

"Wouldn't you be?"

"No, I know Annalise is a good cook. She's a hard worker. Kyle has never once complained about her like he has the other waitresses."

"Do you think she quit?"

"Don't know. I only hope she has what it takes to impress the boss man."

Archie was in total agreement.

****

Annalise loved the kitchen. It was her one place of solace that no one could take away from her. She tied her red hair back on top of her head, washed her hands, put an apron around her body, and got to work on preheating the oven.

This place would be a pleasure to cook in. The oversized windows looked out onto the fields. She had never felt so at peace and prayed they'd choose her for the job.

Checking through the cupboards, she found everything she was looking for.

After Archie had called her to let her know she had a trial to prove herself, she planned the menu for the entire day. Breakfast was a mix of sweet and savory.

The cinnamon buns were already waiting to be put in the oven, since she had started them last night, so they would be fresh today. This opportunity meant the world to her.

Unpacking her goods, she put everything in the fridge, and the ingredients that didn't need to be cool, she placed on the counter.

She didn't know their tastes, so had planned to do waffles, a mixture of sausage and bacon, eggs, and even a compilation of fruit. If she got the job, she would make it her mission to find out everything they enjoyed.

"Don't get ahead of yourself," she muttered to herself.

Annalise wanted this job so badly.

When the ad for housekeeper had first been made available, she hadn't applied as she heard so many people had. Each one had been fired, and then she saw it had been removed. Seeing it in the paper once again, she had called and gotten Archie.

Now all she needed to do was get into the cooking.

It didn't take the oven long to heat up. Then she had the cinnamon rolls cooking and the waffle batter resting. There was plenty of fresh maple syrup, and she poured some into a saucepan to heat up closer to the time.

She opened the door to allow some fresh air in.

By eight o'clock, she was ready to serve, and she got the timing just right as well as she spotted Gabe, Archie, Vinny, and a couple of their ranch workers headed that way.

Everything was still hot.

The scent of cinnamon heavy in the air.

"Score," the ranch hands said.

Hands clasped together in front of her, she pointed out everything she had cooked for them before turning on her heel to leave. She had a cinnamon roll and cup of coffee waiting for her in the kitchen.

The temptation to go and check outside to see if they liked the food was strong. She had tried to offer her skills to Kyle at the diner, but he hadn't been interested. He told her there was only one cook in his diner, and it would forever be him.

Cooking was a passion of hers. As a little girl, she imagined having a large family to cook for. Her home life had never been great. Immediately, a huge wave of sadness washed over her, and she quickly shoved it to one side. Now wasn't the time to think about all that sadness. Her family had no place in her future. She hadn't seen them in years, not that anyone knew the truth of the black sheep of the family, or in her case, the redhead.

With her cinnamon roll finished, she put the plate in the sink, along with her mug of coffee, and got to work marinating the chicken for lunch.

She was thinking spicy chicken sandwiches, with a nice refreshing sparkling citrus drink.

Just as she was massaging the meat, Vinny came into the kitchen.

"Damn, that was some fine food." He rubbed at his stomach.

"You enjoyed it?" she asked.

"Yes. It was so good. As I knew it would be. Those cookies you sent were the best I ever tasted."

She smiled. It was always nice to hear how much her food was appreciated. "Thank you."

"No. Thank *you*."

She nibbled on her lip. "Did anyone else enjoy it?"

Vinny smirked. "Gabe took three portions. There's barely anything left."

"Do you think I can feed your dogs?" she asked. She had heard them randomly barking throughout the morning and had wanted to go and see them. She loved dogs so much. They hadn't been allowed a dog as one of her half-sisters had been allergic.

"Of course. We've already fed them this morning, but talk to Gabe, he'll take you to them."

Vinny winked at her, and she smiled, warmth washing through her body. All three of them were big men, tall and muscular. She'd swear they were brothers, but they were just friends.

Archie stopped by next.

The ranch hands never made an appearance, and finally, Gabe came inside. He made her nervous as her fate was in his hands.

"Vinny said you wanted to see the dogs to feed them." He was so tall and with that stern look on his face, it made her a little afraid. Or turned on. She wasn't so sure.

"Only if you want them to have the food."

"Nothing goes to waste here. I don't have the time or the patience for it. Food is money. Time is money. We work hard here."

"Of course." Should she bow? "Did you, er, did you like the food?"

"It was good," he said.

Was that a compliment? It sounded like a compliment.

"Come on. I don't have all day."

She quickly followed him outside. There were no cages or kennels. "The dogs are able to roam free?"

"Of course," he said. "They sleep in the house. Is that going to be a problem? If you're allergic, you can leave now."

"No. No. That's not what I meant. It's just nice, I guess. I figured some people keep them outside."

"They're good dogs. Good boys. They'll never be locked up outside." He let out a whistle. "Rufus, Barney, get your butts down here."

"Only two?"

"For now," he said.

She watched as two giant German Shepherd dogs came running toward her. At first, she was mesmerized, and then a little terrified as they seemed to be running straight to her.

Chapter Two

Vinny watched as Annalise picked wildflowers behind the barn. The sun highlighted her distinct red hair, the breeze lifting the ends. She was really something to look at. More than that. She made him think of things other than the daily grind.

He'd always been the guy with the smile. He worked. He drank. He partied. Nothing got him down. The truth was that most days he was hanging on by a thread. He just knew how to hide his emotions well. He'd picked up that trick, amongst others, from the countless years he spent in foster care. It wasn't much better than life with his deadbeat family.

Vinny usually focused on getting through one day to the next, but watching Annalise putter around the ranch made him think of things like family and future, which was so unlike him.

"What are you doing with those weeds?"

Annalise gasped and whirled to face his direction. He'd been taking a break in the shadow by the side barn doors. "They're not weeds."

Her face was blanched, her body visibly trembling.

He watched her fidget. "Just teasing."

"I was going to put them on the table for dinner … if that's okay."

"You do whatever you like, sweetheart." He winked, and she immediately looked to the ground. Why was she so jumpy? Vinny wasn't sure if she couldn't stand him or was genuinely shy. Either way, he needed to try his best to keep professional if she was to have a future on the ranch.

She just stood there.

"You okay?" he asked.

Annalise shrugged. "Have you heard anything from Gabe about the job? It's been over a week. I just wondered if he was leaning toward hiring me on permanently or not."

Had it really been that long already?

It seemed cruel to keep leading her on. He'd have to talk with Gabe and Archie. There was no legitimate reason for Gabe to cut her loose. She cooked, cleaned, and did a ton of extras they never even asked for. Life had never been better.

"I'll talk to him. Nothing to worry about."

"I hope so. All my eggs are kind of in this basket."

He tilted his head to the side. "What do you mean?"

"This job, the room, everything. It's perfect. A dream, really. I have to get my stuff out of my old apartment by the end of the week. If this doesn't work out, I'm not sure what I'll do."

"How about I bring my pick-up truck and help you move your stuff out tomorrow?"

"I can't ask you to do that, and I don't want the job out of pity. I shouldn't have said anything." She started to step back, adjusting the wildflowers in her arm.

"Nonsense. Archie will be happy to help. We'll get your stuff tomorrow. No arguing about it."

"Do you think we should? I haven't gotten the all-clear from Gabe yet. I don't want to make any assumptions or make things awkward for him."

Gabe may be rough around the edges, but he wasn't a monster. Even he would have to have mercy on their little housekeeper. Anyway, if anyone was able to talk Gabe into something, it was him.

"We definitely should."

He got up and dusted himself off with his Stetson.

She appeared to visibly relax. "I've never met a Vinny before. That's not a common name around here."

"Well, my birth certificate says Vincent Liam O'Brian, but that sounds too formal. In school, it made me cringe, and at home, it was usually only used before I got a beating."

"I'm sorry."

He frowned, not sure why she suddenly looked so sullen. Then he ran his words back in his head and realized she probably didn't have a fucked-up childhood like he had. He'd stopped feeling sorry for himself a long time ago. "Nothing to be sorry about. I'm not too good at story telling."

"Well, I like both versions. I'll use Vinny so I don't upset you, though."

Vinny walked closer to her until she had to back up against one of the old shade trees close to the barn. "You can't upset me, sweetheart. That ship sailed long ago. Anything you call me will sound perfect coming from your lips." He brushed the backs of his fingers along her jawline, staring into those deep green eyes—but pulled back just as fast. "I'll see you at dinner."

He turned away from her and moved hastily into the barn. Vinny was no good for a sweet thing like her, but every time he was near her, he dreamed of impossible things. Stupid things that weren't meant for a cowboy like him.

Women flocked to him, always had, and he rarely turned them down. He didn't do girlfriends because he tired of them after a couple of weeks. Vinny and stability were like oil and water. The only humane thing to do was keep his distance.

****

Annalise rushed into the house. As soon as she shut the door, she leaned back against it and closed her eyes. She hugged the flowers to her chest and took slow, measured breaths to calm herself down.

Would her past ever leave her alone?

She'd never spent much one-on-one time with the men. Her focus was on keeping her job and ensuring they were happy with her services. She kept her head down and feelings bottled up—but she wasn't blind. All three of the cowboys were ridiculously handsome, tall, and hard with muscle. She'd seen them working the fields, handling the horses, and washing up in the outdoor shower at the end of the day.

Vinny had disheveled dirty-blond hair that was a little too long in the front. When he'd run his hand through it, her heart always skipped a beat. Of all the men, he was the crazy one, always joking and laughing. The risk-taker. But she knew there was a darker side. A sad side. She felt it sometimes, especially in the evenings. Now he'd opened up a little window into his psyche and she'd been right all along. There was much more to the sexy blue-eyed cowboy than what met the eye.

"You hiding?"

Annalise gasped when Gabe came around the corner. Her back was still pressed to the door. "No, just a bit out of breath."

It wasn't too much of a stretch. She definitely wouldn't pass for a fitness model. She'd always been excessively curvy, and a good run would most certainly get her heart racing.

"Dogs aren't chasing you, are they?" He went into the kitchen and poured himself a glass of water from the sink. His skin was sweat-glistened. All three men worked themselves to the bone six days a week. On Sundays, they tried to take it easy, but she could tell they were still antsy to get more things done. There was such an unsettled nature to the men.

"They're little angels with me." She joined him in the kitchen and set the flowers in the oversized vase she'd pulled out from under the counter earlier. Annalise wasn't sure why she felt so damn nervous around Gabe specifically. She assumed it was because he was the decision-maker on the ranch, and she wanted this job more than anything.

There was something about Gabe. She couldn't read him at all. As far as she was concerned, he barely tolerated her. Or outright hated her. If it wasn't for Vinny and Archie, she was sure she'd be out on her ass.

"I'm surprised how quick they took a liking to you," he said. "They're usually slower to trust." Then he stood there at the kitchen island opposite her. He was staring … or was he just lost in thought? Should she respond? Carry on preparing the meal?

She swallowed hard and met his gaze.

"Well, I like them. And I like you, too." Annalise froze in place. Had she actually just said that out loud? She was trying to keep friendly so he didn't fire her, but it sounded more like flirting. Why did she always have to put her big foot in her mouth?

He raised a brow. It was a barely-there movement, but she noticed it nonetheless.

"I'll let you get back to it." He set his glass on the counter and left without another word. Now she was worried about losing her job for being inappropriate. It was never her intention. She just didn't want Gabe to hate her.

As soon as he walked off, she collapsed against the fridge, feeling completely drained. Gabe Cartwright was a lot older than her. She would have claimed she got daddy vibes from him but couldn't, not when he made her heart flutter in the least of paternal ways. A little part of her always hoped he'd rip open his flannel shirt and pull her into a kiss to end all kisses. Her fantasies often got carried away. Living with three of the hottest men in town, it was a constant battle to keep herself in check and professional.

Annalise had trepidation about taking the job in the beginning. Being alone with three men on the sprawling ranch had some red flags. She should be thankful they hadn't tried anything, but most days, it felt disappointing. They had reputations with women, so she was starting to get a complex.

She mindlessly began prepping for the evening meal. Her thoughts were definitely elsewhere. If she could go back in time and keep her mouth shut with Gabe, she would in a heartbeat.

Now Vinny and Archie were supposedly helping her move all her worldly possessions into the house tomorrow. She didn't think Gabe would approve, especially now. This was a disaster. Why couldn't her life have been easier? Why was she so unlovable?

She twirled her hair up into a makeshift bun and pulled out the pots and pans from the lower cupboard. When she stood back up to set some on the counter, Gabe was standing there across the island again. She froze, setting the pots down before she dropped them.

Her heart raced from the scare and the fact it was Gabe. This was it, she just knew it. He'd tell her it wouldn't work out. She'd crossed the line.

"I wanted to apologize," he said.

Silence rained down on them.

"I don't understand…"

"Well, I know you're being paid to cook and clean, but you live here now, so you can't just work from sunup until sundown."

"I really don't mind."

He shook his head. "You need to live your life, enjoy some free time. We have a large property, and there's plenty to explore. Just … be sure to take some time for yourself."

"Okay. Thank you."

What she wanted to ask was if his words meant her position was permanent and she was no longer under probation. It sounded like it to her. She was just so glad he'd come back so she didn't have to overthink what had happened earlier all night long.

He turned to walk away but stopped himself. Gabe ran a hand over his jawline, the scratchy sounded traveling straight down to her pussy. She'd already noticed the five o'clock shadow that complemented his dark hair and eyes. There was a brooding quality to him, a rugged irresistibility. "If you'd like, I could give you a tour after dinner. If you're not afraid of horses, of course."

"That sounds perfect," she said. Did she look as shocked as she felt?

"Good. I best get back to work." This time, he left, and she heard the door close behind him shortly afterward.

She wanted to jump up and down like a schoolgirl. This was like a dream come true. Annalise couldn't wipe the smile off her face as she prepared the meal. Gabe was her one obstacle, the man she feared, the cowboy with her fate in his hands. Now that weight had been lifted off her shoulders, and her future, for once, felt promising.

****

"What are you smiling about?" Vinny asked.

"I'm not smiling." Gabe donned his hat and walked past his friend. He needed to clear their east field and get it ready for planting. There was always something to do, but it seemed keeping busy was as vital as breathing for him. Silence and idle hands gave him too much time to think about things he'd rather forget.

"It's her, ain't it?" Vinny followed behind him. "No man has that kind of smile all on his own."

"Don't you have work to do?" Gabe asked, trying his best to ignore him.

"I need to talk to you about Annalise."

He stopped and faced Vinny. Surely he couldn't see inside his head. There was no way his friend knew about his obsession with the young redhead.

"What about?"

"She's been here long enough for you to see she's an asset. I'm going with Archie to pick up her stuff tomorrow. That all right by you?"

"You both want her on permanent?"

"What do you think? I've never eaten so well in my life."

Gabe knew Archie and Vinny better than they knew themselves. Although he was only five years older, that was a lifetime when they were kids. It felt like he'd raised both men himself. He knew it was the reason they respected him and left the big decisions up to him.

He knew they both had a candle burning for Annalise. That didn't bode well for him. No way would he let a woman come between the three of them. On the other hand, it wasn't natural for a man to live his entire life without a woman. Gabe had visions of what he expected his life to be like at forty-five. It wasn't this.

Maybe a happy ending wasn't meant for him at all. Maybe it was just too late.

"I'm sure all you're thinking about is food." Gabe walked off toward his tractor.

"What's that supposed to mean?"

"You can fool yourself, but you can't fool me.

Just be careful, that's all I'm saying."

"I'm not going to try anything."

"I think you will," Gabe said. "You've dated half the town."

"That's different."

"No, *she's* different. Annalise isn't a fast woman. Not a toy to play with and toss when you're tired of her. You'll break her heart, Vinny."

For once, Vinny didn't laugh or even talk back. He stood rooted in place, even when Gabe looked back over his shoulder a while later. If he couldn't have Annalise, at least he wanted one of his best friends to find their happily ever after with her. He only wished the best for them, forever sacrificing his own happiness and comfort for their well-being. It was all he'd known for decades.

He remembered one night when he was sixteen and the boys were close to turning twelve. Archie had snuck out of his foster home, and Vinny had run away from his again. They were starving, lost, and cold. Gabe had been on his own for a year, mucking out for farmers to make enough for food and a small room in the boarding house. Even at sixteen he was as big and strong as most men, so nobody ever questioned him working and taking care of himself.

Gabe had made them a pot of spaghetti, even though it was all he had. They ate like animals. He felt for them because he was them. They'd met because he'd been friends with Archie's older brother. He died in a car accident two years earlier. The responsibility for Archie kind of fell in his lap. Vinny had been his best friend, so they were a package deal.

He always found it odd that child services never made much effort to get them back in the system. It was hard to place older boys with a violent streak and fucked up by childhood trauma. Nobody wanted them.

Now they were all men and doing well. He was still cooking for them—until Annalise showed up in their lives. It was good to have a woman's presence in the house. It was something none of them ever had. But for once, it wasn't as simple as sharing her. She was a human being, not a tractor or plot of land.

He headed out, blanking his mind as the rhythmic sound of the machinery took over. It took hours to clear the field. Others said it was boring or mind-numbing work, but for Gabe, it was relaxing. He loved the land, the smells, the sights. He was grateful for how far he'd come in life, even if things weren't perfect.

By the time he headed back to the barn from clearing the field, he was exhausted in every way. What he needed was a shower and a good meal. He dusted himself off the best he could then headed into the mudroom. Gabe unbuttoned his padded jacket, hanging it up next to the others, then he began unbuckling his belt. He'd grab a quick shower, then head down for dinner. He could smell the food in the air, and it made his stomach rumble. The boys were definitely right about hiring on Annalise.

"Oh, sorry."

He turned to find Annalise in the doorway of the mudroom, a pink apron wrapped around her curvy body. "It's okay, I'm just heading upstairs for a shower."

"I wanted to tell you dinner's ready whenever you are. I didn't mean to walk in on you like this." Her voice was almost a whisper.

He felt the burn of her gaze on his skin. Gabe was just in his tank top, and luckily, he hadn't dropped his jeans yet. He had to remember it wasn't just the three of them anymore.

"No problem. I won't be long." Gabe gave her a

friendly wink, but her cheeks flushed red almost on cue. He didn't have to be told she was a virgin. They seemed to be scarce in their part of town. That fact only made her more of a temptation.

Chapter Three

Archie looked around Annalise's mundane possessions and was shocked by how little she had.

"I thought women were supposed to be … you know…" He pointed at the room without finishing his thoughts.

"You think women are known for packing six hundred bags for a couple of days away?" Vinny asked.

"Well, yeah, look at this place. This woman doesn't have a whole load of shit, and if memory serves, her family is supposed to be pretty well off."

Annalise was in the other room, gathering stuff together, and he didn't want her to hear him talking about her. The truth was that whenever he used to watch her at the diner, she always looked sad, out of place. People seemed to treat her as if she didn't exist, unless something was wrong with their meal.

He always made the effort to bring a smile to those luscious lips. Damn it, just thinking about her mouth made him want to kiss her. Having her living with them was supposed to make this easier for him, but it was only proving to be incredibly difficult.

Archie's feelings for her were not going away, not any time soon. It was very frustrating. In the past week, their lives seemed to change. The food she cooked was amazing, and he'd stopped visiting the diner simply because she wasn't there to serve the food he wanted. Why go to a place when the person of his desires was living with him?

He wanted to claim her.

Gabe tried to play down his feelings for her as well. Archie had seen the way they had all looked at her, and each one of them wanted her.

Vinny was clearly smitten.

Gabe was in deep.

And himself, he wasn't ashamed to admit how he felt about her—to himself anyway.

"Hey," she said.

Her lips were slightly swollen from all the nibbling she'd been doing. A cute nervous tic of hers. She walked in, and he was enraptured by the sway of those full hips. Did she even realize how sexy she looked?

Archie picked up one of her suitcases, as did Vinny.

"Are you doing okay?" Vinny asked.

"I'm fine. It's just an apartment." She glanced around the room. "I did move in here straight after high school, you know." She blew out a breath. "It's just a place I've called home for a long time." She turned her back, and Archie looked at her space.

It wasn't much by any stretch of the imagination, but he understood what Annalise felt. This was probably her first real home. The one place she called her own.

He left the apartment, heading downstairs to load up the case into the back of the truck. Vinny did the same. Gabe had to check on some fencing back at the ranch, which was why he couldn't come. The landlord was on the doorstep, and Annalise placed the key into his palm and even offered him a smile.

Archie watched as the older man squeezed the key within his fist, looking downright fucking gutted.

He wanted to know what was going on there. A landlord shouldn't look unhappy when they were given a damn key and the room was still in decent shape.

"You see that?" Archie asked, looking toward Vinny.

"See what?"

Annalise came toward them. Her sweet smile

29

stole his heart.

"I'll be right back," Archie said. "I've just got to check on something." He nodded at Annalise, then at Vinny, before heading toward the building. The door was still wedged open. The summer they were experiencing was a fucking killer. He was constantly sweating his balls off.

"Hey," he said, following the landlord.

The man stopped and turned around. "Can I help you?"

"Yeah, I've got a question for you," he said. "Why toss a good tenant?"

"I have no idea what you're talking about." He went to turn away from him, but Archie was already close and stopped him with a hand to his arm.

"Wait, you know what I'm talking about. Annalise was a good tenant. She's been here forever. What's the deal? Is this just about the bottom line? You sell to a builder or something?"

"Look, it's none of my business. I don't get involved in family disputes. This is all I have, and I take pride in offering decent places for people to live at affordable prices. I can't afford all the red tape if the inspectors come down hard on me. I never wanted any of this. I'm sorry for Annalise. I truly am."

The landlord pulled away, and Archie frowned.

"Who wanted you to kick her out?" Archie asked.

"Her stepfather."

Archie nodded. "Is he someone we've got to be worried about?"

"I don't know," the landlord said. "All I know is that he threatened to have me shut down for rental violations, as well as citing the building. He carries a lot of weight, and I can barely put food on the table. At first I didn't believe him, but then I got hit with a city council warning. Believe me, be careful."

"Thanks." Archie didn't see a reason to prolong his meeting with the landlord. He had a hunch about the eviction, and he was right.

He was going to have to talk with Vinny and Gabe, but he wasn't going to worry Annalise, certainly not yet.

"Is everything okay?" Annalise asked as they met back at the truck.

"Perfectly fine." He looked at Vinny, who raised an eyebrow. He gave him the signal that he'd talk about it later.

It was way too hot, and they didn't have A/C in the truck. It was time they headed back out toward the ranch. He turned on the radio and listened to some country tunes.

Annalise's stepfather was making waves, but why? He didn't get it. He knew they weren't close to each other. Anyone could see that.

Why go after Annalise? As far as he knew, she'd been on her own and supporting herself for most of her life.

They arrived back at the ranch and started to unload her belongings.

"It can just go into storage," Annalise said.

She had a couple of bedside tables, a couch, and then a couple of boxes of books, and meager belongings, which included her clothes. Not a lot of stuff.

"Don't worry about it. We've got plenty of room," Archie said.

Gabe headed toward the barn. "This everything?" he asked.

"Yep, everything." Archie and Vinny carried the couch into the living room. They only had three chairs, and even though it didn't exactly fit in with the rest of the furniture, they'd never been one to care about the aesthetic of a room.

Stuff was stuff. When you came from nothing, anything was a prize.

They carried the rest of her stuff up to her bedroom.

She'd only been with them a short time, and already the room smelled like her.

****

"This doesn't have to mean anything," Gabe said.

Annalise had already been settled in for the night, and there was no sign of her. He kind of missed that.

Archie though, seemed to be looking for trouble, which he didn't like.

"Maybe it's something we should take a look into," Vinny said. "Without Annalise knowing, of course."

"Does Annalise even know?" Gabe asked.

He watched Archie run his fingers through his hair with a shrug. "I don't know what she knows. She looked sad about moving though. The old man seemed to like her."

"She might have seen this coming. We don't know her that well. For all we know, she could be a huge bitch."

Archie snorted, as did Vinny. Gabe didn't believe his words either. Annalise was no bitch. He was a good enough judge of character to know that. Whatever her stepfather had against her, it was his own deal.

He leaned forward, resting his arms on his knees. "Look, there's not a lot we can do right now about any of this. We'll keep our ears open and our mouths shut. See what happens. For now, we've got a new housekeeper, so hopefully you assholes will stay off my case." He got to his feet. "I'm tired and we've got a lot to do tomorrow.

Stop worrying about shit that you don't even know what is real or not and focus on what you truly know to be fact. We've got a ranch to run. Not to think about the what-ifs of life. Got it?"

Gabe waited until he got confirmation from his friends before he let them be. He headed upstairs, ignoring the very door their new housekeeper now slept behind.

Damn it.

She wasn't supposed to matter. This was one of the many reasons why he didn't care for a housekeeper. Women were trouble, that was his experience with them all at least.

Ignoring the door and the desire to knock on it, just so he could see her, he went straight to his bedroom. He'd already taken a long shower before Archie demanded his presence downstairs.

There was a book on his bedside table. He made a habit of going to the library once a month to get a title, and so far, he hadn't been able to get into that one. It probably didn't help that their housekeeper had also been with them for over a week. Running a hand down his face, he tried to focus on work.

The fences were an easy fix. Owning a ranch, he'd come to realize that fixing things was pretty much a full-time job. It was all he did, from the fences, to the barns, to the house. He was never too far from any tools, which he didn't mind. He loved to build things. It was the one area of his life where he didn't feel like a constant screwup.

He changed into a pair of shorts and kept his shirt off. The house was still too damn warm. He had the window open in the hope of getting a nice breeze. Nothing.

Lying down on his bed, he picked up the book

and opened it up to the first page.

Gabe read the words, but none of them sank in. His thoughts returned to the woman a few feet away from him.

After an hour of attempting to read, he slammed the book down, got to his feet, and decided to take the dogs out for a walk. There was no way he should be struggling to sleep. Not with the work he did on a daily basis, and yet, that was exactly what was happening.

The floodlights were off when he stepped outside. He took a deep breath of country air. There were more stars than he could ever count lighting up the night sky. Each step on the dry grass created a distinct crunch. They needed rain in the worst way.

The dogs didn't have to sleep in the old barn, but some nights when it was too warm like tonight, they never came in the house.

He came to a stop when he heard a voice.

"I get to stay. Did you hear the news? I'm going to be the best housekeeper ever. I'll make sure to get extra steak for you guys weekly."

Annalise's soft voice permeated the air, and Gabe paused.

She was in the barn?

Why didn't he hear her move around? He swore she'd gone to bed hours ago.

The door was partially open, and he glanced through to see she was kneeling on the ground. She wore what looked like a pair of sweatpants and a negligee.

His dogs were lapping up the attention, and he knew why—she had treats.

How many times had she been in the barn since her arrival?

"I was so worried though. Yeah, I said something silly to Gabe, and I was scared he thought I was flirting."

She groaned. "I bet women are always drooling all over him, and I want him to trust me, you know?" She sighed. "It would be nice to not have to find another job. I love this ranch. Always have. I bet you guys love it too, don't you? Running around, doing whatever you want."

Gabe was worried she might spill some private details, so he cleared his throat and pretended to just arrive.

Annalise gasped and spun around toward him. "Gabe!"

"I didn't mean to startle you."

She attempted to catch her breath. "Oh, it's fine. This is your house and your barn and your land." She quickly stood. "I ... er ... I couldn't sleep."

"It's fine. You don't have to explain yourself. You come out to the barn often?"

Only the flickering light of her lantern gave a soft wash of light to the immediate area.

"Not too often. Just when I struggle to sleep. I love dogs. I always wanted one growing up but was never allowed a pet." She pressed her lips together and then smiled. "I better go inside."

"The heat is distracting me. Do you want to take a walk with me?" he asked.

"Yeah, sure. I'd love to."

He clicked his fingers, and the dogs got to their feet, heading out of the barn ahead of him.

Annalise crossed her arms, but it was too late. He'd already seen the delicious curves of her tits, and damn it, now he wanted to see them better.

Clenching his hands into fists, he remained silent as they walked, side by side, heading toward the first field. The full moon was high up in the sky, casting a gentle glow. All he wanted to do was touch her, to pull her in close, to taste her.

He kept his hands to himself and decided silence was the best course of action.

****

Vinny watched as Gabe threw another bale of hale onto the bed of the truck. The guy had been in a bad mood all day.

"What's up with you?"

"Nothing."

And he was touchy as fuck.

"Did you sleep well?" Archie asked. "Or did a certain housekeeper keep you up?"

Gabe shot a scowl toward Archie.

"What's going on that I missed?" Vinny asked.

"Simple. Our good friend couldn't sleep, went to go and walk the dogs as he often does, only to discover Annalise's favorite spot on the ranch."

Vinny smiled. In the past week, he'd noticed she had a soft spot for the dogs. All of them. She loved them, and he was shocked by how much they appeared to love her back. Not that he minded at all.

The dogs were a good judge of character.

"I had no idea she was in the barn," Gabe said.

"Yeah, but I bet that you enjoyed watching those tits of hers in that silk negligee." Archie smirked.

"The one with the lace?" If it was the one Vinny was thinking of, then he couldn't help but feel a little jealous of Gabe. To be up close with Annalise in her skimpy nightgowns. It was a rare treat. One he wanted to see himself. He'd noticed her penchant for sexy lingerie the first night she stayed with them. In the bathroom, in the laundry basket, he caught sight of the softest lace he'd ever seen, and all he could do was imagine Annalise's ass in them.

He'd gone to bed a happy man, especially after he took care of his raging hard-on in the shower.

Annalise had turned him into a horny teenager. This was bad news.

"The very one," Archie said.

"Enough!" Gabe slashed his hands through the air. "You do realize she's not a woman for you to drool over. She's our fucking employee, and you've got to treat her with respect, not as an object for your desires."

"Is that why you're taking out your frustrations on the hay? You can't have her so no one can?" Vinny asked.

Gabe threw the pitchfork to the ground. "I've got more important work to do. You two can clean this mess up while also thinking about the importance of using your heads and not your dicks."

Vinny watched him go. "He's going to be a pain in the ass."

"When is he not a pain in the ass?"

He shrugged.

Archie grabbed the rake. "Come on, let's get this over with."

"I've never seen him be so defensive like this, have you?"

"I think it's because Annalise is different, you know? She's not like other women," Archie said.

"I want her," Vinny said.

"I know."

"You do as well."

Archie looked up and nodded.

"So, what do we do?" he asked. "Because I bet part of Gabe's problem is admitting that he wants Annalise just as much as we do." He held on to the rake as he glanced back at the house. There was no sign of her. He'd found himself working near the house more often just to catch a glimpse of her.

The heat was killing him, and working out in the

fields would be far more suited to his skills.

He wiped the sweat off his brow.

"Look, I know what you're hinting at, but you might have to accept that it's not going to happen like this."

Vinny returned his attention to Archie. "And what do you think I'm hinting at exactly?"

Archie laughed. "You're not that hard to read, Vinny. It's simple, I know you think there's a chance we can find the one woman that would get us. You don't want any of us to leave or to find families elsewhere. We've been together for so long, all you see is us together in some kind of four-way."

He tensed up.

There was a time he'd teased about them finding one woman between all three of them.

Gabe and Archie were not just his best friends, they were like his brothers. He never wanted to be anywhere they weren't. He loved them both deeply, and knew if they shared a woman, if they fell in love with one woman, then no one would come between them. It sounded farfetched when he thought about it the first time, but now, he only saw the potential future in it.

"I hate to be the one to burst your bubble, Vinny, but that ain't ever going to happen."

Vinny threw the rake down. "You don't know that."

"Do you think one woman could take us three and be happy? Do you really think that would work? The women we've been with wanted us to compete with each other, to fight."

"That's everyone else," Vinny said. "Annalise isn't a whore. I've got to go and clear my head." He didn't want to listen to Archie's negativity.

He found himself storming toward the house, and

as he got to the back door, which led straight into the kitchen, heavenly scents assailed him, as did the sight of Annalise bent over, showing him her beautiful ass.

His mouth watered at the sight alone.

She lifted a slab of what looked like apple pie.

"Vinny, dinner isn't for another hour, isn't it?" she asked.

"Yeah, I just, I needed some water." And the truth was that he needed to see her. Just seeing her was enough to calm his temper.

"I made a pitcher of lemonade. I was going to bring it out to you guys. It's way too hot out there. I hate that you have to work in that heat."

"And yet, you're in here cooking up a storm."

"I've got you boys to feed." She gave him a dazzling smile, and he had this overwhelming urge to kiss her. And more.

Her lips looked ripe and plump. They'd be so soft against his.

She handed him a glass of lemonade. "What do you think?" she asked.

He dropped the glass in his hand, and even though in the back of his mind he heard Gabe berating him for what he did next, he didn't stop. He sank his fingers into Annalise's hair, drew her close, and kissed her, hard.

Chapter Four

So many thoughts flooded her mind.

Fear, passion, relief, and numbness. At first, everything went black and she just savored the feel of Vinny's lips on hers. Then the flashes of anxiety as she contemplated what this meant. She didn't want to sacrifice her job, her life, for this one moment of bliss.

When he pulled back, his hand was still tangled in her hair. He stared into her eyes, not saying a word. She felt awkward and confused as she looked down at the broken glass.

"Don't worry about that. I'll clean it up," he said.

Could she just pretend this never happened? Should she?

"It's okay. Accidents happen."

That was what this had to be. An accident, a momentary slip in judgment.

She felt herself pulling away emotionally. It was what she did, how she'd survived this long. When her mother remarried so many years ago, everything went downhill afterward. Her stepfather was respected and was able to give her mother the life she'd never had. He brought two daughters close to Annalise's age into the marriage, and he didn't want another. She'd only been ten. Her life had never been the same.

Her stepsisters were thin, smart, and pampered. Annalise was always left behind, pushed back in the shadows. Worst of all—her mother condoned the constant abuse and neglect, favoring her new daughters and husband's attention.

Even now, it was next to impossible to accept affection, to believe another person could love her for who she was.

"I shouldn't have done that," he finally said.

"Don't worry about it." She moved away from him and went in search of the broom. What she needed was time to think, to process what just happened. "I'll call you when dinner is ready. Shouldn't be too much longer."

She grabbed the broom and dustpan from the closet, but the moment she turned around, he was there. He grabbed both her arms and got her full attention.

"I said I shouldn't have done that, not that I didn't want to," he said. "Tell me you never want me to cross the line again, and I won't."

How could she? Part of her craved love, craved Vinny. The logical part of her brain and the damaged recesses of her psyche both told her to run. What would Gabe and Archie think? The last thing she wanted was to hurt any of the men, including the one standing in front of her with fuck-me blue eyes.

"I don't know what to say," she said. Tears pricked her eyes.

"I'm not trying to get into your pants, if that's what you're thinking. I know I have a reputation, but it's different with you, Annalise."

"How?"

"I'm forty years old. Playing the field isn't what it used to be. I want more. I never thought I needed more until you showed up."

"But my job. Your friends."

He did a little spin away from her, raking both his hands through his hair. "They'll kill me. Fuck."

"I don't have to say anything."

Vinny looked so distraught that she felt guilty, and he was the one to make the move.

"You know, when we were teens, we used to joke about all kinds of shit, about how we thought life would be when we got older. We talked about sharing one woman." He scoffed. "We were young and stupid."

She swallowed hard. Did he actually just say that? Why did her pussy feel instantly wet and achy? This wasn't good at all.

There was nothing to say. She couldn't even move a muscle.

"How long you going to take? I'm not doing all that loading myself." Archie's voice grew louder as he neared the kitchen. It seemed to pull both of them out of their reverie. "What happened here?"

"I—I dropped the lemonade," Vinny said.

Archie looked down at the mess, then back and forth between them. She sensed something was off, like he knew exactly what had just transpired. Did he? Could he?

"And you're just going to stare at the mess?"

Vinny glared at his friend. "I was about to clean it up when you walked in." He took the broom from Annalise and began gathering up the glass bits from the tiles. "I'll be out in a minute."

"Is there any more lemonade?" Archie asked.

She took a breath to keep calm. "Yes, of course. Would you like some?"

"I'd love some."

Annalise turned back to the pitcher and poured some into a clean glass. She handed it to Archie, but he put his hand over hers rather than taking the drink. Did he notice the shake in her hand?

"You okay?"

She nodded, not trusting herself to blurt out something inappropriate.

"Vinny, you say anything dumb?"

The last thing she expected from Vinny was more silence. Why wasn't he lying or covering up what just happened? Instead, he set the broom against the wall and left the house.

Archie took the glass and watched his friend leave. He exhaled once they were alone.

"What did he say?" Archie asked.

"Nothing."

He drank his lemonade. She watched the movement of his throat. He had some rough stubble along his jaw. After he slammed the empty cup on the counter, he looked her straight in the eyes. "Did he ask you for a foursome?"

She gasped, then slapped her hand over her mouth. Her cheeks felt like they were on fire. It may be surprising for them, but she was a virgin, and all this talk about sex was way out of her comfort zone.

****

He knew it.

The second Archie saw Annalise and Vinny in the kitchen, he knew he'd gone and opened his big mouth. Archie told his friend that sharing a woman wasn't realistic and to put the thought out of his head. Vinny was proposing some twisted ménage relationship where all four of them lived happily ever after and Annalise had no qualms about fucking three cowboys.

It was a fantasy. Nothing more.

Now he expected Vinny had ruined everything. By the tension in the room, Annalise was probably ready to walk.

"It was an accident. I don't blame Vinny."

"So he did say something?"

She shrugged. "He was just talking out loud. Remembering dumb things you all did when you were teens."

Archie wondered what Vinny had said. How much had he revealed about their fucked-up lives? Some things were better kept in the past where they belonged.

The last thing he wanted was for Annalise to think less of him or judge him for his past.

"He needs to learn to keep his mouth shut. I can't even count how many times he's made a mess of things by saying too much."

"You all were close."

"Still are," he said. "Not everything was bad. He has his good qualities." Archie remembered the many times they'd only had each other to lean on. Vinny was a lightning bolt, a hot wire. He'd follow them to hell if he thought they were in trouble. "I was a runt in high school. Vinny got suspended more than once beating up guys who picked on me."

"*You* were a runt?"

"Sometimes bad experiences are the catalyst for change." He'd packed on muscle after having a late growth spurt. Years of working on the ranch and hitting the home gym made him unrecognizable from the skinny kid he was in his youth. Many of those deep-seated insecurities still remained, no matter how much he'd remade himself as an adult.

He didn't feel worthy.

Annalise was too damn good for a scrap like him.

"Well, you've done well," she said. "I never would have known."

The way her gaze roved up and down his body made his cock harden in his jeans. He didn't need this right now. Archie was trying to be the voice of reason, but now he was sinking as low as Vinny. His thoughts were in the gutter. He blamed his friend for putting these twisted thoughts in his head.

"I just wish I'd had the ability to protect myself when I was a kid, you know?" He scrubbed a hand over his face. God, he was a fucking downer. "But no need to dwell on the past."

"I don't mind listening," she said. "It's nice. I'm not used to having anyone to talk to."

"You have all of us."

She smiled, but it wasn't happy. "I know, but I work for you. There's a line I know not to cross. I'm good at keeping professional, so you never have to worry."

Archie frowned. He didn't want a robot working for them, but he also knew he wanted more from her than just cooking and cleaning. How would he survive living with Annalise underfoot without screwing up? Vinny had even less willpower than he did.

"I don't mind. We're not assholes. I mean, you live here, too. Is it so wrong to be friends?"

"What kind of friends?" she asked. "Foursome friends?"

He felt the color leach from his face.

This time her smile reached her eyes. "I'm just joking."

Archie laughed along with her, but deep down, there had been a smidge of hope. Vinny's fantasy was getting under his skin.

He leaned over the counter and beckoned her closer with a finger. When she was close enough he could smell her subtle perfume, he whispered, "Don't take Vinny too seriously. He speaks before he thinks. I don't want him to upset you."

"You don't have to worry, Archie. I'm a good judge of character."

She did work at the diner for years. A lot of different characters probably passed through. But she wasn't that good at judging because she couldn't read him. He yearned for her, felt like a rider constantly pulling on the horse's reins. What would her skin feel like? How soft were those curves of hers?

How long could he play the nice guy before he fucked up a good thing? Vinny would probably be the one to send her running first.

"I wanted to ask you something," he said. Archie was pulling at straws, trying to think of any reason to stay close to her just a little bit longer.

"Okay."

Damn, her innocence was a turn-on. She looked up at him with those big doe eyes while he was thinking the most unholy of thoughts.

"Next month is Gabe's birthday," he blurted out.

Her mouth fell agape. "What? Really?"

He shrugged. "It's kind of a secret because he hates the thought of growing older. He's already five years older than me and Vinny."

"Oh. No celebrating?"

She sounded so disappointed, and that wasn't his intention. "I was hoping you could help me make a cake. A nice homemade one. He loves strawberry best."

Her smile lit up the room. "Yes! I'd love that. We can get the ingredients together. He may not want a fuss, but everyone wants to be remembered, don't they?"

He nodded. "Yeah, I guess deep down everyone wants to matter to someone."

Archie had his two friends, and that was it. For a long time, that wasn't enough. There had been a deep-seated desire for a parent's love, but that went unfulfilled. The foster system fucked him up in more ways than he cared to imagine.

That was the past.

This was his life now, and lately, he started wondering if he'd ever be satisfied. Annalise made him yearn for more. The status quo with his two friends wasn't enough. He needed a woman, a family, a future. Just thinking about spreading his wings at this age made him well up with guilt. Gabe and Vinny were all he knew.

"I know exactly what you mean. I've spent so many years believing I only amounted to anything if I had someone in my corner," she said.

"I don't get it. You're a Davenport, aren't you?" As soon as he finished speaking, he remembered what her landlord had said about her stepfather. Maybe things weren't so rosy in her life after all.

"Yes, I'm a Davenport. It's just a name. And it's not really mine at all."

"What does that mean?" He craved to get closer to her, to heal all her sorrows. Archie felt a soul-deep bond or connection between them, even though they weren't much more than strangers to each other at this point.

"My mother remarried. Davenport is his name."

"Don't like the sound of it?" He was pushing for more and hoped he didn't cross too many lines.

She started chewing on her lower lip. Normally, he found it sexier than fuck. Right now, it made him sad. "I guess you could say I was the black sheep. He had two daughters and—"

She stopped talking, right in the middle of a sentence. The house felt quiet. Too quiet.

"Annalise?"

After a deep breath, she continued. "I'm sorry. I'm thirty years old. These memories shouldn't still cut me so deep. I don't even like to hear that name."

He reached out and ran a hand over her hair, gently tugging her closer. He kissed her atop the head. "I don't need to know if it upsets you. I'm all for blocking out the past. It's all I've done."

"It's not healthy," she whispered.

"Survival isn't pretty."

She looked up at him, his hand still in her hair. "Shouldn't we want more?"

He swallowed hard. Archie wanted to tell her he wanted it all. Wanted to make all her dreams come true while chasing away her demons. Instead, he was a coward and nodded.

****

He'd promised to give her a tour of the property on horseback. All they'd done so far was take a quick walk by moonlight. It had been a disaster. Gabe had been avoiding her because she unraveled him every time he got alone with her. He prided himself on his self-control, and Annalise was his kryptonite.

Showing weakness wasn't an option, and trust was something he'd given up on decades ago. A woman like Annalise could break his heart if he lowered his walls too low. They had a good thing going on at the ranch. She'd only make things more complicated, get the three of them fighting for her attention.

Yet, here he was, planning on taking her out on a late-night horse ride. It crossed too many boundaries to count, and he knew damn well his willpower would be tested.

He'd been waiting for her outside while she ran inside to grab a shawl. There was a nip in the air at this time of evening despite the brutal heat by day. The crickets chirped in an endless chorus throughout the fields. He breathed in deeply, loving his time of night. He felt free, young, like anything was possible.

"Are you sure this is a good idea?" she asked.

"What can go wrong?"

She smiled and carefully plodded through the thick grass shrouded in shadows. "I thought you'd changed your mind about the tour," she said. "I didn't want to push about it because I know how busy you always are."

"It slipped my mind after dinner yesterday. But I'll make it up to you tonight. How are you getting along now that your stuff is all moved in?"

"Good. I always told myself I wouldn't put all my eggs into one basket, so it's a little disconcerting, but I couldn't be happier."

"The boys behaving themselves around you?"

She giggled. "For the most part."

Gabe turned around and stopped dead, leaning against the paddock fence. He raised a brow. "What did they do? No, what did Vinny do?"

"It's nothing. Honest. I was just playing around."

"No, there's more to it," he said. Everyone had been acting off since yesterday, and he hadn't been imagining it.

"I thought you guys were close. Don't you tell each other stuff?"

"Not when it comes to you," he said. "What did Vinny say?"

She ran a hand through her hair. "It was just some comments about a foursome. How he couldn't imagine being away from the two of you. It was a silly thought from a long time ago. I thought he mentioned it to you."

"No, that, I'd remember."

What was Vinny doing? He wanted a housekeeper, but he'd single-handedly scare her off if he kept talking garbage. Why couldn't he keep his big mouth shut?

"Forget I said anything."

He realized he was still standing there blocking the path, his brow furrowed and hands clenched. It was too easy for him to zone out into thought. "I'm sorry he insulted you. I'll talk with him."

"He didn't insult me."

What did that mean? She'd brushed off the comments or did a foursome pique her interest? He was about to delve into an area he had no business visiting. "Sharing a bed with three men doesn't make you skittish?"

"Not if it was the three of you."

Fuck me.

Was she playing with him again? Was this a test? He wasn't sure how to respond.

"I don't think an innocent little thing like you should be entertaining such thoughts," he said. Gabe swore he could hear his own blood rushing through his veins. Every sense was hyperaware, along with his cock.

"Why? Is it because I'm not your type?"

Where did this siren come from? He was used to Annalise keeping quiet and only appearing to serve their food.

"You're exactly my type."

Her lips parted slightly. "That's hard to believe. Maybe you've been alone on the ranch too long."

"You think I don't know what I want?"

"Word is you only care about working," she said.

He scrubbed a hand along his jaw. "Because that's all I have. All I know. I've sacrificed my life for Vinny and Archie."

"So, you're not allowed to be happy? You act like you have one foot in the grave."

He shrugged. "I'm forty-five and live alone with my two friends. Things can only go downhill from here."

"If you don't look for something, you won't find it."

He looked her up and down before staring deeply into her green eyes. What was it about this girl that drove him crazy, made him want things he had no right wanting? He'd seen how Vinny and Archie looked at her.

This entire situation was a clusterfuck.

Gabe smirked. "You telling me I should look for love?"

Chapter Five

Why didn't it surprise her that Gabe would think of someone else?

Annalise wanted to kick herself. Ever since Vinny had mentioned the foursome comment, she couldn't stop thinking about it, and now, she couldn't even focus on keeping her thoughts out of the dirty gutter. At this rate, she was going to end up without a job.

"You should look for whatever makes you happy," she said.

"Working makes me happy."

She stopped and looked at him. Gabe raised a brow. "Does it?"

"Does what?" he asked.

"Does work make you happy or does it just fill up the time?"

He folded his arms, and she saw the twitch of his lip.

"What about you?"

"What about me?" she asked.

"Are you happy with just working? That's all I see you do around here."

"I … I like working, I do. It's not what I want to do every single day of my life."

"Tell me, Annalise, what do you want from life?" he asked. "Do you hope to find love someday?"

His words sounded like he was mocking her, which she hated. It was on the tip of her tongue to lie to him, to keep her feelings to herself, but she knew that no one ever learned from lying.

"One day, yes. I hope to find love. I'd like to have a man who loves me, and to be a mother. Is that so farfetched to even think about?" Annalise asked. She expected rejection, insults, or even laughter.

"You're angry."

"No, I'm not angry." She pressed her lips together. "I just know that finding love is not as easy as people think it is. It's hard and..." She shrugged. "There aren't many lucky people out there." She wrapped the shawl around herself. "Can we take a raincheck on the tour? It's late and I want to get up early tomorrow."

She didn't want to be around Gabe.

"Annalise, wait," he said.

She'd already turned on her heel and was trying to leave, but he seemed determined to stop her. He reached out to grab her arm, and she didn't attempt to fight him. There was no reason to.

There was no fear for this man, unlike her stepfather. Part of her expected to have a chip on her shoulder for all men, but they were clearly different people.

"I didn't mean to upset you," he said. "I'm royally screwing up here."

"You haven't upset me. I'm fine. I'm just tired."

"To be honest, I've never been good with women. Can't say I've ever been in a serious relationship. Most women have wanted to tear me, Vinny, and Archie apart. I don't know why. Maybe jealousy. Maybe it was some kind of game to them."

"I'm so sorry," she said.

"It's ... no ... I've never stopped wanting love, but when you live the life I have, and the women I've been with, I know that love isn't that easy to find. Kind of seemed like a figment of the imagination. There are so many people who want to fuck with my way of living. Who want to tear me apart, and this ... family, I can't do anything to jeopardize it."

"Which is where the foursome thing comes in,

right?"

"That was one of the reasons why we had talked about sharing one. It was one of the only ways we saw of this ever working. Our friendship isn't common. No one understands but us."

"One woman together with all three of you?" she asked.

"Yes. I know it sounds crazy."

"I have to go."

"Annalise, I'm sorry. You don't have to leave."

She had already started to walk away. She needed time to think, and she'd only get the space by being alone. With Gabe speaking so … normally about the prospect of sharing one woman, she was struggling.

She had never considered sharing three men.

They're never going to pick you, anyway.

Was she more insulted or angry that it would be another woman?

Annalise rubbed at her temples, trying to expel the horrible thoughts trying to hurt her. Insecurities that had been instilled in her ever since she had moved in with that horrible stepfamily.

Not once had her stepfather acknowledged she existed. She'd been an inconvenience. Nothing more. Being second best had destroyed her from the inside out.

Her stepfather took great pride in seeing her mother embracing his daughters while never giving her own the time of day. It wasn't fair, but her mother never saw a problem.

For years, he had forced her from one corner to another. Attempting to trap her in a bad situation. She had no idea why.

Rushing to the house, she charged through the kitchen, ignoring Vinny and Archie's questioning looks, and ran straight toward her bedroom. She closed the door, flicked the lock into place, and moved back until her legs hit the bed. She collapsed.

The thought of belonging to three men didn't repulse her. Should it?

Gabe's suggestion had freaked her out on every level because she didn't expect to have any feelings about it at all, and yet, here she was.

A virgin she may be, but she wasn't blind to her own feelings. She knew what she wanted more than anything.

She craved love.

Needed affection.

At the same time, she didn't know how to accept it. After too many years of going without, she didn't find it easy to accept love.

They didn't say they wanted you, dimwit. They were talking to you as a friend.

Tears filled her eyes and she stared down at her hands.

"Your mother never wanted you."

"She wished it was you in that grave instead of your father."

"You're a useless piece of trash."

Annalise swiped at the tears, trying her best to remain calm, even though it was the last thing she felt. She was holding on by a thread.

Taking a deep breath, she slowly started to let it out. One long inhale, and a slow exhale. This was what she got used to being back at home, when she heard them acting like a family downstairs, and she'd been ordered to stay in her room until they were ready for her. They never called for her. She always remained in her room and was never allowed out. Out of sight, out of mind. This was the way her life had been for so long.

Covering her face, she began to sob into her

hands. Years upon years of neglect swamping her. She'd never felt so utterly alone in life.

She knew these feelings should have been dealt with long ago, but she couldn't stop them. Annalise had been ignoring her own pain for far too long. The moment she started to cry, there was no stopping it.

****

Gabe ignored the questioning looks from his friends. Archie and Vinny were already on their feet as he entered the house. Annalise had looked so damn miserable after he told her what they had planned.

He didn't get it.

It wasn't like he had asked her to belong to them, and if the idea repulsed her so much, she could have said no or told him to fuck off. She was probably disgusted with them.

"What's going on?" Vinny asked.

"You! What the fuck did you do earlier?"

"I didn't do anything. Annalise was happy, laughing at everything I said. You're the one who sent her home crying. What the hell was that about?" Vinny asked.

Gabe's hands clenched into fists. He wanted to hit something, and he knew going after his best friends wouldn't be the ideal solution. They didn't deserve his anger.

"Just tell us what happened," Archie said. "Come on, we all said a woman would never get between us. You starting now?"

"She hasn't gotten between us," Vinny said. "But you know what, I want her between us, so I'm going to say it. I want her." He pointed toward the stairs.

Gabe shook his head. "No."

"No, I didn't say I wanted her for myself," Vinny said. "She thinks I was joking around with the foursome comment, I wasn't. I want her, and there is no stopping me. Tell me right now, Gabe, that you don't get rock hard thinking about her. That you don't want to bend her over the nearest chair and fuck her so hard that she screams your name."

Gabe ran a hand down his face, trying to calm his anger. It was impossible to do so while he thought of Annalise, bent over the sofa, her beautiful, curvy body on display as he spread the cheeks of her ass open and began to fuck her. She would take all of him.

This wasn't good.

He wasn't supposed to be giving in to these thoughts. Annalise was their employee.

"You're fucking busted," Vinny said. "You can act the cold bastard to me, but I see what you want."

"Fuck off, Vinny."

"Gabe, I see it too. You want her," Archie said.

He looked toward the staircase, and as he did, they were all so incredibly silent. Gabe heard it. The soft sounds of sobbing. If they hadn't stopped arguing, he wouldn't have known.

Without a word to his friends, he moved toward the stairwell and began to walk up.

"Gabe, what the hell are you doing?" Archie asked.

"I'm going to go and make this right."

He didn't look back, but kept on walking, turning toward her door as he got to the top of the steps. The door was closed.

Putting his palm against the wood, he couldn't think of the words he needed to make any of this right. She probably thought he was a dirty bastard.

He gritted his teeth, annoyed with himself for causing her any harm.

The sobs he heard hurt him, twisting a knife

through his heart as he listened to them. Annalise should never have to cry. Certainly not because of him.

He twisted the door only to find it wouldn't budge. She'd locked it.

"Annalise, open the door," he said. "Please."

"I can't."

"Baby, please," he said.

There was silence. Then he heard some movement.

"What do you want?" she asked.

"I need to see you."

There was a second of hesitation before he heard the lock unclick. Annalise opened the door, just slightly, and he took full advantage. He gripped the door, and she was no match for his strength as he pushed it open, but he made sure not to jerk or jar it in any way, to keep her safe and protected. She released a little gasp and stepped back.

He entered her bedroom and closed the door behind him.

She'd been crying, no doubt. Her lips were swollen, her eyes red-rimmed.

"You need to leave," she said.

"I'm not leaving until you tell me why you're crying."

She sniffled. "It's none of your business."

"Is it because of what we talked about downstairs?"

"No, of course not."

"Then tell me, because right now, I don't know how to make this right and I feel like I'm the one responsible for making you cry. I can't stand it. I feel worse than shit. You're a good person."

This made her laugh. "I'm not a good person."

He frowned. "What?"

She shook her head. "Please, I'm sorry. I'll move out tomorrow."

"You don't have to move out," he said.

"None of this is because of you," she said. "I get it, okay? I do. I'm not good enough to even be thought of for your foursome. I know it's completely laughable. But I don't want to be around when you find your perfect woman. It would be awkward."

Gabe held out his hand. "What?"

"It's fine. You don't have to worry about insulting me. I've been told plenty of times that I'm not good enough. No man will ever want to settle down with a woman like me, except—"

Anger, hot and sharp, rushed through every part of his body. It was so fast and intense, at first, he couldn't believe what he was hearing. "Who the fuck told you that?" he asked.

She licked her lips and shrugged. "I've been told it most of my life. You don't have to be upset. The woman you fall for, she's going to be one lucky woman."

This wasn't a play.

Gabe saw her and knew in his gut that she was speaking from the heart, the truth, and it annoyed him. He was ready to fucking kill the person who had made her feel this way. How could she even believe it? She was gorgeous, sweet, and sexy as fuck.

He stepped toward her and stopped when she moved back. "I need you to tell me who told you this kind of shit."

"It's fine, Gabe."

"No, it's not fine. Not on my watch."

She took a deep breath, and he saw the tears building in her eyes again. "I'm really tired."

"It's your stepfather, wasn't it?" he asked.

Her lip trembled.

He couldn't recall meeting that son of a bitch, but when he did, Gabe was going to make sure it was a meeting the asshole never forgot.

Gabe moved toward the door, wanting to give her space. He stopped and looked toward Annalise. "Just so you know, you're the only woman we want, Annalise. Make no mistake about that. Vinny, Archie, and myself, we're all fucking smitten with you."

****

Vinny shoveled more hay onto his fork and tossed it into the waiting truck with some force. He was pissed off.

"Are you imagining that was Gabe's head?" Archie asked.

Gabe had taken his horse and had started the day by going out and checking fences. Vinny and Archie were shoveling hay once again. Not that they needed to, but Vinny had to do it. If he didn't, he was going to kill Gabe.

He'd been flirting with Annalise, slowly getting closer to her until he found the right moment to steal that kiss. She'd been skittish, as he imagined she would be. She was terrified of losing her job, and to a point, he got it, he did, but she needed to know he wanted her, so badly.

He ached for her. It felt like he'd been waiting all his life for her, and then Gabe went and threw away his hard work.

After he'd gone to Annalise's room, she had stopped crying, but Gabe had then told them what happened. As far as Vinny was concerned, he'd messed up his grand plans.

"He's always meddling when he's not supposed to," Vinny said. He speared the fork into the hay.

"Gabe's always been like that."

"And I've appreciated everything he's done for me. I love the guy, okay, but right now, I'm pissed. We're not monks, Archie. Does he expect us to live alone forever?"

"What do you think Annalise is going to do?" Archie asked.

Vinny had stayed up all night guarding the front door in case she attempted to run away. He'd been relieved she hadn't tried to leave. But his back hurt like a bitch this morning from the uncomfortable position on the sofa.

"Not a clue." He didn't know what she was going to do. That morning, breakfast had been ready for them, but she hadn't been around. A quick glance through the kitchen window showed she was in the vegetable garden they had all spent months carefully organizing. She avoided them.

Gabe drank his coffee, ate his breakfast sandwich, and left.

He'd been slowly stewing over what had happened, and Vinny hated the silence.

"I need a drink," Vinny said.

He'd been shoveling hay for most of the morning. It was back-breaking work, and he needed a drink, and he also had to see Annalise. She was on his mind all the time, and not knowing if she was okay was starting to worry him.

As he got to the house, he knew instantly she wasn't home.

He entered the kitchen and saw a pitcher of lemonade with a note.

I've gone to the shop for some ingredients. I will be back before lunch.
Love, Annalise.

"Has she left?" Gabe asked, coming up behind him.

"No. She's gone grocery shopping."

"Why didn't she ask any of us for help?"

"I've got a couple of clues." He poured himself a drink of lemonade.

"You're pissed at me."

"Totally." Vinny leaned against the counter.

"You're not even going to try to hide it?" Gabe asked.

Vinny snorted. "Got no reason to. Now if you'll excuse me, I've got some shoveling to do." *And I'm imagining it's your head.*

"Vinny, I want her as well," Gabe said.

"I know. I know we all want her. I know there's a fucking chance we could finally get our dream, but instead of helping, you sent her to her room crying, and now I'm pissed off at you." He stepped out of the kitchen.

Gabe called his name, but he didn't stop until he heard someone else clear their throat. He stopped and turned, seeing an older man, probably in his mid-fifties. The wrinkles at the corners of his eyes and lips gave it away. His hair also had some white streaks running through it.

For some reason, Vinny just knew this was Annalise's stepfather.

"I'm Raymond Davenport, I would like to talk to you about Annalise's employment." He removed his glasses and straight away, Vinny didn't like him. There was something about this son of a bitch that rubbed him the wrong way. It wasn't the expensive clothes or the designer watch. It was the man's eyes—cruel and entitled. The bastard was smug, the kind of man he couldn't stand.

"What about it?" Gabe asked.

Vinny moved closer, showing support, as did Archie. They were a team, a unit, even if he did want to shovel hay and imagine he was hitting Gabe with his fork over and over again.

"I would like you to terminate her employment." He reached into his jacket pocket. "I am more than happy to compensate you for her time, and of course the money you have already paid her."

"Why?" Gabe asked.

"Pardon me?"

"You expect me to fire a perfectly good employee just because you say so. Why?"

"It would be in your best interest to do so. Annalise is a troubled girl. I am only looking out for her."

"Looking out for her?" Gabe asked. "Now, the last time I checked, when you force someone to fire another, remove them from their home, and genuinely make their life miserable, that is not *looking out for someone.*"

"Just give me a number of what it would take for you to get rid of her," Raymond said.

"Nothing. No amount of money is going to get her away from us." Gabe moved closer. "Annalise belongs to us."

Vinny couldn't see Gabe's face, but whatever Raymond saw, it was enough for him to take a step back while also putting his checkbook away.

"I see. You should have taken the money. You're making a huge mistake."

"Get the fuck off my property, right now," Gabe said.

"I'm assuming you don't know who I am, but you

will regret this," Raymond said.

The man didn't linger. He turned on his heel and walked right over to his overpriced SUV.

"What the hell was that all about?" Vinny asked.

"I know what the stepfather is trying to do," Gabe said.

"What?" Archie asked.

"He's trying to push Annalise into a situation where she has no choice but to beg him for help, and when she has nothing left to lose, the son of a bitch is going to strike. Raymond Davenport wants his stepdaughter," Gabe said.

Chapter Six

Three weeks later

Archie backed up one of the livestock trailers up to the corral. With his arm propped out the window, he maneuvered the truck until he was close enough to lower the ramp. He cut the engine and hopped out, grabbing his Stetson before slamming the door shut.

Life on the farm had been tense lately.

He'd barely talked to his friends, and Annalise did her job without saying more than two words. How long could they all live in fucking silence? Vinny's foursome fantasy, Gabe pissing off Annalise, and the stepfather appearing out of the woodwork were all creating a living nightmare. He wished they could go back in time and undo all this bullshit.

Today he had to load twenty sheep and goats, ten piglets, and an assortment of their so-called "cute and cuddly" herd for a local event. They rented out animals for events, fairs, and seasonal petting zoos. They were always looking to maximize their revenue on the ranch. Keeping all their eggs in one basket had gotten them flat broke a couple of times, so they'd learned from their mistakes. He'd never forget the year they lost almost everything during a drought when they'd put everything into cash crops. Every field had to be plowed over. It was a disaster.

"I thought you might want to take your lunch since you'll be gone a while."

He turned to find Annalise approaching him with a brown paper bag. There was no one else around at this end of the ranch.

"That's for me?"

She nodded, outstretching her arm.

"Mighty thoughtful of you. Who told you I'd be

gone?"

"Gabe mentioned it after breakfast."

He hated that they said exactly what they needed to say and not a word more. How long would he be able to keep going on like this?

"I should be back by dinner, but these little fluffballs can be a real pain in the ass." He set the paper bag on the fender and reached into one of the pens and pulled up one of their long-haired baby bunnies. Her eyes lit up and, for the first time in years, he didn't resent the little fuckers.

He walked closer to her and handed her the bunny.

"It's so cute." She cuddled in up to her chest. "And soft."

"You should see all the critters we have in these barns. I'd be happy to show you."

He could hope.

She smiled. It was slight but unmistakable. Annalise shrugged, which he took as a yes.

"This lot is heading out to the town's birthday celebration. It'll take me quite a while to get them all loaded."

Annalise peered into the pens. "They don't look like too much trouble."

"Mostly the piglets. They're slippery little buggers. Why do you think Gabe and Vinny disappeared after breakfast?"

"They stuck you with the workload?"

He leaned against the split-rail fence, taking off his cowboy hat to wipe his brow. "I'm not complaining anymore." Archie stared at her, hoping she could sense his emotions. He had this connection with her and couldn't explain it himself. For the past few weeks, he kept wondering if she'd disappear one day. He wished he knew how she felt about everything.

She looked to the ground. Was she shy, insecure, or brushing him off? Damn, he couldn't read her at all.

"If you're free for a while, I could use some help."

"From me?" She still had the bunny cuddled up between her cleavage. "I don't know much about farming or animals, just cooking."

"Don't sell yourself short. You have a knack with animals. I've seen you work wonders with the dogs, and that baby bunny looks quite at home."

He was jealous of the bunny right now. Annalise had the most luscious tits he'd ever seen on a real woman. He could imagine what she'd look like naked in vivid detail.

"I'll help if I can," she said.

"Excellent." He took the bunny from her, returning it to the secure pen. "Let's start with the worst of them, in case you decide to change your mind later." He winked.

"The piglets?"

"That's right."

"No changing your mind now," he said. He walked around the back of the barn, the shadows providing a brief reprieve from the heat. Her footsteps were close behind. Before he rounded the corner, he stopped abruptly. Her hands briefly pressed against his back to keep from crashing into him. That simple touch felt like the most intimate thing in the world.

Archie turned around, leaning against the barn wall. "I've missed talking to you, Annalise."

She nibbled on her lower lip.

"Things have been ... uncomfortable. It's our fault, not yours. I wish we could start over. Can we start over?"

This time, she looked him in the eyes rather than the ground.

She shrugged. "We just made something out of nothing. I want to work here, but I hope you all won't keep avoiding me like the plague."

"We just kind of thought you hated us."

"I don't hate you. I have no reason to."

"Gabe said some things…"

"I know he didn't mean anything he said. People make mistakes."

Gabe hadn't made a mistake. They all wanted to have a ménage relationship with Annalise, but it wasn't worth losing her completely. Maybe she'd never be on board with their twisted desires or maybe it would just take time. He was willing to wait.

He ran a hand along his jawline, realizing he hadn't bothered to shave the past few days. It was hard to give a shit when his emotions were all over the place. "You'll really forgive us? Forgive me?"

"I'm helping you with the piglets, aren't I?" Her smile was sweeter than sunshine.

"Right." He pushed off from the barn wall and continued to the pigpen around back. "Okay. There they are. You get four and I'll get four. Fair?"

"Sounds fair."

****

Annalise felt like a huge weight had been lifted from her shoulders. She hated the silent treatment. It reminded her of life back home when she was younger. Everyone loved to pretend she didn't exist. Or to ignore what was happening under their noses.

It was one of her triggers as an adult, so hearing Archie talk to her beyond the required pleasantries was refreshing and healing. This all started weeks ago because of a misunderstanding—or so they wanted her to believe. Gabe had said outright that they all wanted her, wanted to keep and share her between the three of them. It was too much to process and next to impossible for her to believe.

Being alone with Archie brought back her deep-seated feelings. His brilliant blue eyes stared down at her in the sunlight, and the scruff on his face made him even more masculine. Part of her wanted him to blurt out it was all true, to demand she agree to their foursome. But it felt like more a fantasy now that they were talking civilly again.

He opened the gate for her, quickly closing it behind her. She was already wearing her rubber boots.

"Sneak up behind them and grab them around the middle. They're squirmy little things, so make sure you don't let go once you get a grip," he said.

Annalise liked pulling her weight around the ranch. They paid her well and gave her room and board, so she liked to do more than just cooking and cleaning when she could. How hard could it be to transfer a few cute, little piglets? And they were cute. In fact, all the animals at this end of the ranch were adorable.

She took measured steps, the muck suctioning around her boots, making it difficult to walk. Annalise wanted to appear capable and not a damsel in distress, but as soon as she lunged forward, her boots stayed rooted and she fell face-first into the mud.

Did Archie just laugh? She swore she heard it for a second.

She struggled to her knees and tried to push the muck off her arms, but she only made it worse.

"Need some help?" he asked.

Annalise answered through clenched teeth. "I'm fine." She managed to get up with unexpected difficulty, then lifted her boot before going after the next piglet. She was already a mess, so what did it matter now?

Worse than the thick mud was the smell.

When she snagged the rear leg of a piglet, it began to squeal and struggle. She brought it close to her chest as not to drop it and calm it down. Even in her predicament, when she looked down at its little face, she couldn't help but smile. It was so small and cute.

She hadn't realized she'd zoned out while bonding with the little pig. Annalise turned in Archie's direction. "I did it."

"You certainly did." He had one booted foot on the fence rail. No man should look that sexy in a pair of blue jeans and t-shirt. She knew for a fact all those muscles were hard-earned and not from a gym. "How about the rest?"

"I think you'll be much faster than me. One is enough for today." She was already in desperate need of a shower, and it was a long walk back to the house. Wrangling pigs was not her forte.

She passed the squirming piglet to Archie, and he placed it in a large crate in the back of the trailer. He vaulted over the top rail of the fence into the pen with ease and began snatching up piglets like it was his full-time job—she supposed it was. Archie was a seasoned cowboy, and she watched in awe as he finished up the job with barely any muck on his boots.

Once loaded in the crate, he brushed off his hands and turned to her.

"What just happened?" she asked.

He laughed. She noticed a cute dimple on his right cheek when he smiled, a mix of boyish charm and rugged masculinity. Was Gabe telling the truth, even a little bit, about the three of them being crazy about her? A flicker of hope burned inside of her.

"I have a few talents."

She had no response because her mind was in the gutter. Annalise just stood there like a clueless, filthy beast.

"The other animals are much easier to handle, but you can't be comfortable the way you are. Once that mud dries, you won't even be able to crack a smile."

She could only imagine what she looked like. "I guess I should head back and clean up."

He frowned. "No need." Archie beckoned her to follow him to the barn. He ducked into a stall and came out with a green hose. "We should get the worst of it off here."

"Okay." It sounded more like a question because she wasn't crazy about the idea of being hosed off with cold water.

"Close your eyes. You've got a second skin."

She did as told, using her hands to cup over her eyes. The first blast of cold water made her gasp, but it wasn't as bad as she expected as the heat outside was brutal. It was almost refreshing and very nice to feel the gross mud wash off.

Archie was thorough, moving around her, soaking her clothes right through. She began to feel self-conscious, realizing her clothes would be clinging to her explosive curves. Would he be able to see clear through her blouse?

When the water stopped, she opened her eyes, running her hands through her wet hair to get it off her face. "This wasn't how I planned my morning when I came out here with your lunch bag."

"That's what makes life fun, isn't it? The unexpected. The crazy memories." He was standing close to her, within an arm's length.

"I'll definitely remember today for the rest of my life."

He closed the short distance between them, reaching out to adjust the collar of her shirt. When she glanced down, her blouse was completely transparent and practically glued to her body. Even her satin bra was soaked, showing her dark areolas and hard nipples.

Her face heated with embarrassment. Her cheeks were likely redder than her hair.

When he didn't move his hand, his fingers caressing her neck, she looked up to make eye contact with him. There was no more humor in his eyes, only need, desire. Her pussy instantly clenched, moisture flooding her already wet panties.

She was thirty years old, but this was the first time she'd been in this position. The range of emotions coming alive inside her confused her, but she undoubtedly wanted Archie. Should she resist? She didn't want to refuse him anything right now.

"You're stunning," he whispered.

Annalise had never been called stunning. His compliments made her entire body tingle. She was soaked and covered in slop only minutes earlier, but his words still sounded sincere.

She swallowed hard, leaning into his touch. His hand was warm and strong.

"You're all I think about, Annalise."

"Archie…"

"Every word's the truth. I should have said something earlier, but I didn't want to scare you off. We've been trying to behave ourselves, to give you space."

"I don't want space."

He supported the back of her head and leaned down to her level, kissing her hard on the mouth. She saw it coming, but it still shocked her. Archie kissed her like it was his last kiss. It felt like love even though that was impossible.

Passion.

Desperation.

Need.

Her knees became weak. The entire world went away, and all she could do was feel, all her senses magnified. He moved his hands down the length of her body. His touch was possessive, not delicate.

"We should get these wet things off you," he said. The words were whispered close to her ear, then his tongue traced the shell of her ear, making her shiver.

She didn't protest, allowing him to slip off her blouse. He immediately unfastened her bra, her big tits dropping heavily without the support. Archie growled as he used both hands to cup her breasts. When he bent over to suckle her pebbled nipple, she cried out, sinking her fingers into his dark hair. He took what he wanted, and she was ready to give him everything.

Being outside in the open air, the risk of being seen, even though slight, added to the eroticism. She'd never been this naked in front of anyone or outside of the privacy of her bedroom.

"You're even better than I imagined, baby." He mauled her, cupping her ass and pressing her into the fence. She felt the hard ridge of his cock against her stomach, which sobered her slightly. She was a virgin. Did she want to lose her virginity against the side of a pig pen?

"Does this feel good?" He cupped her crotch with his big, strong hand. The rush of forbidden pleasure stole her inhibitions. She dropped her weight into his hand, wanting more, needing more.

"Please, Archie."

He groaned, nuzzling her neck until the sound of a truck approaching had him pulling away.

****

Gabe drove out to the far barn to tell Archie the township wanted to add llamas to the order, but instead of finding him loading sheep and goats into the trailer, he found a nearly naked Annalise. Her tits were huge and absolutely perfect. His cock instantly hardened in his jeans.

What the fuck was happening?

He finally noticed Archie standing right next to her. Was the bastard making a move on his own, trying to claim her for himself? They'd all agreed to be on their best behavior. Gabe had barely spoken with Annalise the past few weeks. It was too damn awkward, and he couldn't begin to guess what she thought of him.

Annalise crossed her arms over her chest as he got out of the truck. She looked like a doe in the headlights, not moving a muscle. He knew his friend well enough to know he'd never force himself on any woman, and she certainly didn't look terrified. More guilty.

"What's going on out here?" he asked Archie.

"What does it look like?"

"It sure as hell doesn't look like loading critters. Annalise looks wet and naked. Don't tell me you have an explanation for this one," Gabe said.

"I fell in the mud trying to catch a pig," Annalise offered. "He was hosing me off."

"Looks like he hosed your clothes right off your body." Damn, she looked good, absolutely edible. "Let me drive you back home."

"We don't need help," Archie said.

He crossed his arms over his chest. "From what I can see, your truck is hooked up the trailer and you have a deadline to meet."

They had a stare off until Annalise's voice cut the silent tension.

"I don't want to go home yet."

When he turned to her, he felt like she'd stabbed a knife to his chest. She'd chosen Archie.

"And you should stay too."

That surprised him. Even Archie's mouth fell agape.

"And what do you need me for?" he asked, not wanting to assume anything.

She shrugged, but he saw the devil in her eyes.

He reached for her hand, and she actually took it. Gage tugged her close, their bodies nearly touching. He stared down at her, using a curled finger under her chin to get her full attention. "Did Archie touch you? You let him play with these beautiful tits?"

She nodded.

He used a finger to paint a soft line down her neck to where her cleavage started. "Do I get a turn?"

She moved her arm covering her nipples and grabbed a handful of his shirt. "I thought this was what you wanted," she said.

"You have no idea, baby girl."

Annalise nibbled on her plump lower lip, and he was a goner.

Chapter Seven

Vinny had been trying to figure out how to fix what he'd fucked up. Everything had been going great with Annalise, and then he had to open his big mouth, and now none of them were talking. Unless he counted Gabe spewing out all kinds of instructions and the endless list of jobs to do, conversation had been pretty stilted.

He was tired, bored, and plain old lonely. He didn't understand why the guys were so pissed. Annalise had been interested in his fantasy. She wanted, no, he didn't believe just wanted, but craved all three of them. For the first time since thinking about his wish, he truly believed it was a possibility for all of them to be happy. To find happiness with each other.

Running fingers through his hair, he pulled his horse to a stop at the trough filled with water. It was so fucking hot that he and the guys always made sure there was plenty of water around for the animals. He slid off his horse and ran his hand down the body, then smiled. He loved this horse.

The sound of a feminine moan drew his attention.

"What's that do you think, buddy?" he asked.

He didn't believe in tying the horses up as they were so well trained. He gave his horse a final pet, then turned toward the sound. There was no mistaking Annalise's voice. His cock hardened at the sound. He was no fool and knew exactly what that sound meant. His woman, their woman, was being touched.

Vinny advanced toward the sound with an added kick of excitement about the prospect of what he would find. His heart raced, and when he came around the side of the changing barns, his cock went into fucking hyperdrive. Annalise was completely naked with Archie on one side of her, and Gabe on the other. His friends were touching her, their hands everywhere. She moaned as Archie cupped her tits while Gabe's hand rubbed between her thighs.

Vinny stayed frozen in place for some time, a mix of shock and awe. He cleared his throat. "Am I interrupting something?"

Annalise's eyes opened, and he saw the arousal in her gaze as she stared right back at him.

She licked her lips and shook her head. "No, you're not interrupting."

"You want Vinny to join us as well, baby?" Archie asked.

"It was his idea," she said.

The way she sounded. The soft scratchy tones of her voice, it made him hard as fucking rock. This was the best fucking scene he'd ever witnessed, and as his friends stood touching their woman, he couldn't look away.

Her tits were nice and large, exactly the way he liked them, and they made his dick ache.

She had curves in all the right places, and he needed her so badly. He closed the distance between them and cupped her face, tilting her head back. "You want this? You really want us? No games?"

"I don't know how to play games, Vinny. I don't want to lose any of you. I ... I'm so new at this."

"We're not going to let you go. Not now. Not ever. You will belong to all of us." He slammed his lips down on hers, wrapping his arms around her back, stroking down toward her ass, and gripping the soft, supple flesh. He drew her closer, and Gabe must have moved his hand as nothing got in his way from feeling her, chest to hip against him.

Was this all a dream? Had he passed out from heatstroke in the field?

He slid his tongue across her lips, tasting her, hearing her slight moan before he plundered into her mouth. She cried out, and he smiled against her lips.

"I think this should be moved into the house. I don't want anyone else seeing what's ours," Vinny said.

"Good point."

Gabe scooped her up and brought her to his pick-up truck, settling her in the passenger seat. He and Archie hopped in the back. Within minutes, they were back at the house. He was just pleased they didn't have many guys working that day. No one was close by to see their woman. Vinny adjusted his cock as it started to feel way too tight.

They led Annalise upstairs, still completely naked and not trying to hide it.

After entering the bedroom, he stood at the doorway and watched as Gabe kissed her deeply.

Her body was a thing of beauty, just as he knew she would be.

"I want a piece of that action," Archie said, pulling his shirt off over his head and stepping in close.

Gabe broke the kiss, and then Archie had taken her lips. It was oddly erotic sharing a woman. He didn't feel the discomfort he assumed would be present with a foursome.

And not one to be outdone, Vinny tugged his shirt off and approached Annalise. She stopped kissing Archie and turned toward him.

"Is this what you wanted?" she asked.

"Yes, fuck yes." He ran his hands down her body, touching her everywhere he could get. She was so fucking sexy, so magical, and all his. He pushed her hair off her shoulders, wrapping it around his fist so he could tilt her head back and finally take the kiss he wanted.

This time, as he brought the kiss to a stop, he

trailed his lips down her body, going toward her tits. He cupped each large mound, drawing them together, and he started to tongue her nipples, sliding across each peak.

Annalise arched up against him, moaning his name.

"Let's get her on the bed," Gabe said.

Vinny let her go and watched as she was helped onto the bed. Gabe stepped between her thighs, and he moved so he had a good view as his friend took one of her ankles in his grip and began to slowly kiss up the inside of her leg.

She gasped as he advanced closer toward her pussy.

Vinny wanted a taste of her, but he held himself back, merely watching this time. It was surprisingly satisfying watching her enjoy herself.

Annalise's eyes were closed as she wriggled beneath Gabe's mouth. So wanton. So needy. He never thought he'd see her like this.

He couldn't look away as Gabe opened the lips of her sex, and then his tongue danced between her slit, gliding across her clit.

As he stroked back and forth, Annalise wriggled against his tongue, moaning their names, all three of them.

Vinny looked across the room at the other side of the bed to see that Archie had removed his clothes and already had his hand wrapped around his dick, ready and waiting his turn.

****

Annalise tasted even better than Gabe could have imagined, and over the past few days, he'd been doing a lot of that. The very thought of Annalise not speaking to him left a giant hole deep inside him. He didn't know how she'd done it. How she'd gotten under his skin, and now, he couldn't imagine life without her, and he didn't want to.

He was so pissed off with Vinny for speaking aloud about his fantasy. A four-way. But there was nothing better in the world than sharing one woman with his two best friends.

Her moans filled the air as he stroked his tongue across her clit, sliding back and forth before taking the swollen nub into his mouth and sucking on it hard. Not too hard, but enough to make her thrash beneath him on the bed.

Gabe gripped the cheeks of her ass and pressed his face against her cunt. She tasted so damn good, but he was never one to be a greedy bastard.

Lifting up, he looked between Archie and Vinny and smiled. "Who else would like a taste?"

Both friends moved closer, if that was even possible. Seeing as they'd gotten naked, he stood up and stepped back, joining them as he removed his jeans. He'd already kicked off his boots the moment he entered the room.

Archie was the next to move between Annalise's legs. Gabe knew the moment Archie's tongue touched Annalise. He just couldn't keep the sounds of his pleasure at bay.

She cried out.

Her hands went to the sheets beneath her, clenching them within her fists.

Minutes passed, and then Archie moved out of the way for Vinny. They were all so very used to sharing. It felt almost natural.

Again, more moaning, and Gabe's cock was so damn hard. Pre-cum leaked out of the tip. He had no choice but to wrap his fingers around the length, stroking from the base right up to the tip, and down again.

He needed to do something to alleviate the pressure. Gritting his teeth, Vinny stood up. Annalise still hadn't found an orgasm.

"You have to go first," Vinny said.

Gabe tensed up. "What?"

"You've got the best kind of control," Archie said. "You can make this good for her."

He hadn't really thought about who would go first, not with Annalise. Their conversations about sharing had always been without much conviction, seeing as the women who'd entered their lives before her hadn't been the kind of women you'd want to fuck.

With Annalise's legs spread, her beautiful body on full display, she looked even better than in his dreams, and there was no way Gabe could turn her or this opportunity down. She was so fucking … gorgeous.

Stepping close to the bed, he put his knee on the edge and moved back between her spread thighs. He slid his hands beneath the cheeks of her ass and pressed his face against her soaking wet cunt.

He began to flick his tongue across her clit, keeping his attention on her swollen nub and feeling her slowly start to climb, almost hitting a fever pitch of pleasure as she began to rock toward her release.

"Please…" she begged.

Gabe didn't stop. He took her right over the edge, with Archie and Vinny listening, as he finally brought her to completion.

Over and over.

She cried out, her moans the sexiest music he'd heard in a long time.

He pressed a kiss to her clit as he let her go and immediately moved between her thighs. Gripping his dick, he worked his length between her slit, and then stared into her big green eyes. There was no looking away. She stared a little in awe, and he couldn't resist smiling.

"Tell me to stop," he said.

Annalise shook her head. "I want it all."

She sounded so needy, so desperate for his cock. He'd never been so turned on in his life. Gabe didn't even know if he had the ability to go slow. It had been so long since he'd been with a woman, and it had been even longer since he'd been with a woman he actually cared about.

Annalise was so different. Did she even realize how much she meant to them? How crazy she made him feel? He doubted it.

With his gaze still locked on hers, he eased the tip of his cock down to her entrance. No condom. He didn't want anything between them.

In the back of his mind, something niggled at him. Something important he should have remembered.

He tensed up, wanting to please her, to give her exactly what she begged for. He slammed balls deep inside her, her walls squeezing the shit out of his cock.

The moment he tore through Annalise's pussy, he knew something was wrong. She tensed beneath him. The sound of her painful cry broke through the veil of pleasure that had crashed down around him.

She was in pain?

He'd caused that.

She shoved at his chest. He grabbed her hands and pinned them to the bed.

"What is it? What's the matter?"

"Holy shit," Vinny said.

"We should have known," Archie said.

"Well, can you give me the fucking answer?" He didn't have time for cryptic shit. Annalise was in pain, and he needed to figure out what to do to stop it.

"She's a virgin," Archie said.

The moment the word was said, Gabe just knew. There was no doubt. He'd even suspected it when she first moved in. She was so tight, and tears leaked out of her eyes.

Staring down at her, he couldn't help but be amazed. "You're a virgin?"

She nodded. It was a small motion, but one he caught without any trouble at all.

His cock had torn through her hymen.

She was a virgin.

His first ever one, and at that moment, Gabe knew she was going to be the only virgin he ever had. Annalise was his now, and he was never going to give her up. Not to anyone.

Her legs were circled his waist, gripping him tightly.

"How is that possible?" he asked. He let go of one of her wrists to stroke her face. Annalise had been given to them, and they were going to treasure her always.

****

Archie waited for the explosion to happen. There was no way Gabe was going to be happy with this revelation. Gabe didn't handle shocking news well, but there was no anger, no sudden accusation. Just his best friend stroking Annalise's cheek, so tenderly.

"I didn't mean to hurt you."

"It's … I've never … this is all new."

Damn it, they should have known. The innocence was not an act with Annalise. It was all real. It was why they had never seen her at bars in town, or out on dates, and he should have known.

He'd kept an eye on her for some time now, and he made it his business to know all kinds of information about women he wanted to fuck, and she had always been at the top of the list.

Finally getting Gabe to agree to a housekeeper had been a great victory in his mind.

Hands clenched at his sides, he watched Annalise as she turned her face toward Gabe's palm.

"I wish you'd told me. I would have made it a lot better for you," he said.

She smiled. "This is perfect. I'm sorry if I scared you."

"I didn't want to cause you pain."

Archie watched as she gave a little wiggle. "No pain. Not anymore. Promise."

Gabe chuckled, and at this, Archie looked over at Vinny, who had a goofy smile on his face. Archie figured he must have the same kind of look because that was exactly how he felt.

"Are you ready for me to fuck you now?" Gabe asked.

She nodded. "Yes. Please, yes."

"So polite."

Gabe tensed up as he eased out of her virgin pussy. Archie couldn't look away as he watched his friend's cock suddenly appear. He noticed the small smear of blood that showcased Annalise's virgin state of just minutes ago.

Gabe eased in slowly, cautiously, riding her with more control than he'd be able to manage.

Annalise cried out, arching up.

Gabe knew what he was doing, and Archie didn't want to look away as he began to change tempo, going fast, then slow, taking his time, making love to Annalise, and fucking her at the same time.

Archie took mental notes of everything she liked. Each thrust drove her higher. How she cried out slightly more when he swiveled his hips, hitting just the right spot deep inside her pussy.

Wrapping his fingers around his length, he started to work his cock, watching the scene before him. How fucking beautiful it was, seeing Annalise come apart.

Partway through, Gabe sat up, his dick still inside her. He licked two fingers, and placed them between her thighs, and this brought Annalise to life as she started to wriggle on Gabe's cock.

Archie could no longer stand back, and he moved in closer, going to one of her heavy breasts and stroking the curve of her tit before putting his lips on her nipple.

"Fuck, yeah, do the same, Vinny. I bet she loves having all three men touching her. They wish they were me right now, Annalise. Their dicks are rock hard because they want to be inside you. Don't you, boys?" Gabe said.

He and Vinny moaned their agreement. The sound loud enough for her to hear. He sucked her nipple into his mouth, and the temptation to bite down just a little bit was strong, but he held himself back, giving her time to get accustomed to having her tits sucked by two men.

She cried out, her hands going to their hair, sinking into the length.

"Fuck, I can feel her. She's getting tighter." Gabe growled as Annalise came. Archie knew he was already addicted to the sounds she made. They were soft, sweet, and drove him crazy.

He was ready to come, but he held himself back, counting to ten as Gabe began to rock inside her. Gentle at first, and then it was like his friend realized he was inside Annalise, and he began to fuck her, pounding into her pussy, making her scream and beg. Archie was so close. He had no choice but to stop or he was going to come right there.

Gabe's breathing changed, and Archie lifted up, watching. Vinny did the same.

"I'm not going to last," Gabe said.

Archie groaned and began to work his cock, feeling his own release starting to roll up through his body, to take control, and he was right. There was no stopping it.

The moment he came, his cum spilled out of the head, sending milky droplets onto Annalise's pale skin.

Gabe wasn't too far behind as he slammed deep inside Annalise.

Archie was very much aware their best friend hadn't worn a condom, and seeing as moments ago she'd been a virgin, he doubted she was on birth control.

Vinny was the last one to join them, his cum joining Archie's on her stomach.

They were all panting for breath. It was the only sound in the main bedroom. Archie stared down at Annalise and saw the flushness to her cheeks.

He couldn't help but wonder what was going on inside her head.

They were silent. It took a while to recover their breath.

Gabe's hands still gripped her hips tightly.

The weight of what they had all just done started to hit him. There were no regrets, at least for him. This was what he'd been hoping for. To Archie, this was a dream come true.

"I think…" Gabe stopped. "I think it's time you told us what's going on with your stepdad."

Annalise tensed up. "What?"

"Your stepfather stopped by the other day, and he wanted us to get rid of you. To kick you out. Even offered us money. I want to know what that son of a bitch has against you, and why."

Well, leave it to Gabe to ruin a perfectly sweet moment.

Chapter Eight

The moment Archie groaned in irritation, Gabe knew he'd fucked up. He'd never had much tact when it came to feelings or expressing himself. He was a workhorse and not used to flowery words ... or claiming a woman with his two best friends.

"Way to ruin the moment," Vinny said.

He'd just taken Annalise's virginity, and they were all still reveling in that beautiful afterglow. He should have bided his time and brought up her stepfather another day. Any other time. But his mind was scattered in so many new directions. Knowing he'd claimed Annalise made him feel a new possessive energy, and he didn't want anything or anyone coming between them. He'd defend and protect her for the rest of his life. She was his now—theirs.

"It's just a question," he said.

"One that could have waited until tomorrow. Or never," Archie said.

"She's our responsibility now. Her problems are our problems."

He rolled over to his side and tucked Annalise in close. With the fog of sex gone, her eyes were alert, and he could sense a mix of embarrassment and awkwardness. That was never his intention.

She smiled at him when he made eye contact. "My past is my past. I don't dwell on it. All I care about is now."

"The past came knocking at our door. No one's allowed to screw with your life," Gabe said. "I won't allow it."

She wriggled awkwardly against him. "He's just a control freak. I haven't seen him in years. I'm sure he wished my mother never had a daughter when they were married. When he started crossing the line, even my mother wouldn't believe me. In fact, I think she hated me even more."

"What line?"

Annalise shrugged. "Weird touching, inappropriate comments, and just a sixth sense that he wanted more than a stepfather should."

"I knew it," Archie said.

"The moment he opened his big mouth, I knew he was bad news," Gabe said. "Nothing to worry about, darling. You have us now."

She smiled, and it melted his heart.

"I like the sound of that. I've never really had my own family. I've always been an inconvenience."

"That nonsense is over. You're the only woman in our lives, and you belong here on the ranch with us."

Vinny sat on the edge of the bed. "None of us have ever really had a family. We've only had each other. Now we have you. Everything feels right for once in my life."

"I thought for sure Gabe would ruin everything for us," Archie said.

He turned and scowled at his friend. "There's nothing wrong with being slow to trust. It only proves Annalise is exactly where she's meant to be."

Gabe kissed her atop the head.

Today was a good day.

"I can't believe this is real," she said. "I mean, I thought about it, but it didn't seem possible."

"The four-way?" Vinny asked.

"Yes, that."

"We're not normal men," Gabe said. "We're used to taking care of each other. It's only natural we share everything."

"What about jealousy? What will people think? I

feel like this is all bound for failure." Annalise sat up, pulling the sheet up to cover her nudity.

"Don't worry the outside world. It never did us any favors," Archie said. "As for us, why would we be jealous if we all get to keep you? Now women can't ever break us apart because there's just one to share."

"It's just that most men tend to be possessive of their woman."

"You haven't seen nothing yet," Gabe said. He grabbed the back of her neck in a secure grip and held her close. "You belong to us now. Only us." Then he kissed her to seal the promise.

All her worries and concerns were sobering, but she didn't know Archie and Vinny like he did. They were one well-oiled machine, and now that he really thought about it, this arrangement couldn't have worked out better.

****

Annalise walked down the aisle at the grocery store, checking the ingredients off her list. Even though she was officially dating all three cowboys she worked for, she still enjoyed cooking for them. It was more than a job now. It was her new lifestyle and a dream come true.

All the men had kept their distance the past few days since Gabe took her virginity. It had been fast and sudden, and she should have told them the truth about her lack of experience, but it had still been one of the most memorable days of her life. They'd been all over her, touching, tasting, and kissing. It felt like an erotic wave washing over her and she was helpless against them. They knew exactly what they were doing, and that experience and control was an additional turn-on.

They never asked about her stepfather again. She couldn't believe he was still trying to control her life all these years later. He was a freak, and she wanted nothing to do with him or her mother. That chapter of her life needed to close. She wasn't asking him for money or help, so why couldn't he just leave her alone and focus on his precious wife and daughters?

Vinny had dropped her off at the grocery store before going on a feed run. He'd probably be back soon to pick her up, so she picked up the pace. Tonight, she was going to make her famous chicken pot pie from scratch. The guys loved it, and making them happy was her new motivation in life.

After paying for her food, she pushed her cart outside to the parking lot and waited at the front of the store. It wasn't as hot today, but it was still early, so it was deceptively pleasant. She twirled her hair to one side, watching the clouds drift across the crisp blue sky. Vinny promised to take her to the coffee shop before heading home, and she looked forward to it. She was very easy to please, but Gabe, Archie, and Vinny always seemed to go above and beyond to make her happy.

A short time later, the rumble of the old pick-up truck drew closer. Her entire body lit up when she saw him pull in front of her. He hopped out, slamming the door behind him. He was so tall and strong. His work boots were only partially tied, and his dirty-blond hair was disheveled from wearing his cowboy hat. He ran a hand through it as he neared her, and it was the sexiest thing.

"Ready, darlin'?"

She nodded, reaching in the cart for one of the bags.

"You leave that to me."

Annalise didn't dare argue. He treated her like a princess. She took a seat in the passenger side as he loaded up the back with the groceries.

When he got back in the driver's seat, he smelled like burning wood and the great outdoors, a masculine scent she associated with him. He put his right hand over hers, steering the truck with the other. "Now what?"

"Are we still going to the coffee shop?"

"Right. I did promise you that, didn't I?" He turned and flashed her a smile. Vinny was crazy handsome with piercing blue eyes. When the sun hit his face at just the right angle, she saw the ocean when he looked at her.

"You did."

His hand moved to her thigh, his fingers dangerously close to her intimate parts. Her entire body tingled in anticipation. "We could make a pit stop before the coffee shop."

"Where?"

"Maybe one of the back roads, away from prying eyes."

Her mind immediately went to the gutter, her pussy clenching in deep waves. "For what, Vinny?"

"I haven't spent much time with you lately. Thought we could have a little one-on-one time."

She wasn't even sure how a foursome should work. Was it normal to spend time with each man separately or was it breaking some kind of code? She didn't want to screw anything up. "Okay…"

He put both hands on the wheel now and steered the truck to the outskirts of town, away from all points of civilization. She watched the view out her window, wondering what he had planned for her. Once they were surrounded by nothing but hay and wheat fields, he turned onto an abandoned driveway, the remnants of an old century barn the only thing around for miles.

As soon as he cut the engine, silence settled in. He leaned closer, the bench seat creaking. "Can I kiss you?"

She wet her lips, then nodded. Would her voice even work right now? The moment felt surprisingly intimate and sexually charged. He ran the backs of his fingers along her cheek before kissing her lips. The kiss grew in intensity quickly, and they shifted closer to each other without breaking contact. She wanted him all over her, wanted him to fuck her like Gabe had. She was so ready, the fear of her first time a recent memory.

He growled, his hand slipping under her blouse.

"I've been dreaming of you since before you moved onto the ranch. My beautiful Red."

She felt herself blush slightly. Her hair had always been a torment for her. She'd been constantly teased in school for her red hair, freckles, and extra pounds. But Vinny liked everything about her. He made her feel beautiful for the first time in her life.

Vinny ran his thumb over her nipple in slow circles.

"That feels so good," she whispered.

He took her hand, placing it over his jeans at his crotch. His erection felt like lead, and she salivated just thinking about all the wicked things they could do together.

"That's what you do to me, Red."

She loved the fact she could arouse him. Yet her insecurities kept nagging her deeper thoughts. Why couldn't she just accept this happiness without expecting it all to implode?

"Vinny?"

"What is it, baby?" He kissed down her neck.

She tried not to become lost in the heat of the moment. "Have you shared many women with Gabe and Archie?"

"None."

He kept kissing and leaning into her.

"How do I know this will last?"

She bit the inside of her lip after speaking. The last thing she wanted to do was sabotage their brand-new relationship. But she desperately craved reassurance. Stability. A place where she was loved unconditionally. This time, he pulled away, his eyes narrowed. "Where is this coming from?"

"I've only known the three of you a short time. I don't want to be the flavor of the month."

He let out a puff of breath, a sound between being shocked and insulted at once. "Annalise, we don't do anything lightly. We're all in. If we say we love you, we play for keeps. You belong to us. Now. Forever. We may have made a lot of mistakes, but one thing we are is loyal."

She nodded.

"Does that scare you?" he asked.

"No, it's exactly what I needed to hear." She tugged him closer and kissed him deeply, all her pent-up nerves turning sexual.

Vinny pulled himself away, opening the truck door and slipping out. "Come here."

She slid along the bench seat toward him. Once she was outside on her feet, he squatted down and pulled her leggings and panties all the way down to her ankles. She stepped out of them and he immediately hoisted her up against the side of his truck. He took up the space between her legs.

Annalise wrapped her arms around his neck as he fiddled with his belt. They were hungry for each other, kissing like they'd been separated for a lifetime. He reached between them to position himself. In one smooth thrust, he filled her pussy full of cock. She cried out from the sudden, delicious intrusion. He pumped his hips, fucking her like a machine, the entire truck rocking.

"Such a tight little pussy." He combed his fingers into her hair and pulled hard to the side. Vinny kissed the exposed side of her neck, sucking and nipping. She felt stuffed full, so completely dominated. He pounded into her hard, his muscles tense. She ran her hands all over his shoulders, arms, and back. He was toned and built like a man should be. This was a working cowboy, rough, dirty, with no apologies. All three men had a reputation for being reclusive and dangerous. And she had one deep inside her, taking away the ache, sating her every desire.

"Tell me you're mine," he said.

"Yes!"

"Pull off your shirt, I want to see my tits."

She struggled to get her blouse off as he continued to pump inside her. It felt naughty being out in the open air so close to the road. She was stark naked now, with Vinny screwing her against the side of his old pick-up truck. It was perfect.

"Feed it to me."

Annalise had overly large breasts. They'd been a hindrance until she saw how much her cowboys loved them. She held one up between them, and he leaned down as best he could and wrapped his mouth around her nipple. The dual stimulation had her hurtling dangerously close to orgasm. She wanted this day to last forever.

"So fucking edible," he mumbled. Vinny adjusted his grip, one hand under each thigh. "Come for me now, Annalise. I want to feel you milking my cock."

An inhuman burst of energy had him ramming into her so hard and fast that there was no way she could hold back the inevitable wave building deep in her cunt. She detonated, crying out as her pussy contracted around him over and over. The wash of erotic pleasure made her eyes roll back in her head.

Vinny continue to claim her until he groaned, filling her with his seed. He slowed, then finally stopped. His chest heaved, his head resting on her shoulder. She kissed his forehead.

"Are you still taking me for coffee?" she finally said.

He chuckled. "Yes, Red, let's go get that coffee."

****

The diner was busy. When he checked his watch, he realized it was lunch hour. He could sleep for hours after his foray with Annalise, but she wanted to go for coffee so he'd walk it off.

They entered the diner, the bells chiming against the glass behind them.

"For two?" the waitress asked, a tray of food in her hand.

Vinny nodded.

A few minutes later, they were led to a window booth at the far end of the diner. They sat opposite each other. He beckoned for both her hands once they were settled. Her skin was soft and milky white.

"Maybe we could have a bite to eat, too," he said.

"As long as you don't ruin your appetite. I'm making chicken pot pie tonight."

She was such a good cook. His mouth salivated just thinking about dinner. "Promise."

"So how long have the three of you been together?"

"Oh, Lord, it's been a lifetime. More than twenty-five years? I'm not even sure."

"No family?" she asked.

"Not worth keeping in contact with."

He really didn't want to hash out his fucked-up childhood. It was one of those things he tried to forget, not reflect on. He'd spent more time in foster care than with his mother. That bitch didn't deserve anything from him now that he was finally making a life for himself.

"Same for me, I guess."

"I know about the stepfather. What's all that about?" he asked.

She shrugged. "My mom remarried when I was a kid. Her new husband had two daughters from a previous marriage. For some reason, my mother took to them and brushed me off the best she could. I was unwanted and I knew they'd be rid of me if that were an option."

"I can't even begin to understand that."

"I spent most of my time away in my room, out of sight, out of mind. My stepsisters were given every opportunity. I was tolerated until I finally moved off on my own."

He squeezed her hand and took a cleansing breath. "And him?"

She looked down at her lap. "He wasn't a father figure, let's just say that and be done with it."

"Yeah, let's not talk about family anymore," he said. "The past shouldn't be allowed to have so much power over us."

"I thought I'd left it all behind. I've been taking care of myself for a long time. I don't know why my stepfather would show up and try to sabotage my life."

"He's an asshole."

Vinny would love a few minutes alone with that bastard.

"I agree."

They had burgers and coffee. Both of them stopped talking about the past and focused on happier things like the zoo animals they kept, and how he wanted to take her on a horse ride through the forest trails one day soon. They even talked about Christmas on the ranch, and he described how the snow would blanket the land and the old wood stove that would keep them warm. Talking with Annalise came so easily, like he'd known her for years. He supposed that was what happened when a man fell in love.

After paying the bill, he gave her a wink. "We'd better head home before they think I've kidnapped you."

She smiled and slid out of their booth ahead of him.

"I'll be out in a second. Just going to use the bathroom," he said.

When he exited the diner a couple of minutes later, he saw a couple of men he'd never seen before. They were tourists, probably heading to the next rodeo town.

Both of them looked to be in their mid-thirties, and they had Annalise cornered.

"Come on, sweetheart, just tell us your name."

Vinny bounded down the few steps and headed straight to the men with no hesitation.

"Problem here?" he asked, getting between them and Annalise.

"Nothing that's your business, big boy."

He smirked. "Well, *she's* my business."

"She's got a mind of her own. And she can choose who to go home with tonight."

As he lunged forward, all he could remember was Annalise screaming his name. His Irish blood ran hot, and all he saw was red. He punched the asshole with the big mouth in the face, and he kept pummeling, ignoring the pain in his knuckles. When the other guy tried to step in, Vinny took him down to the dusty ground, rolling with him before straddling the fucker so he could dish out more punishment.

All he kept thinking about was the fact they'd disrespected his woman. His territorial nature ran off the charts and he barely recognized himself.

It was Gabe's booming voice that pulled him back into reality.

Chapter Nine

Several hours later, Gabe still paced the length of the living room. Every few seconds or so, he'd stop, glance over at Vinny, shake his head, then carry on pacing.

He was so pissed off.

No, disappointed.

At this very moment, he couldn't even put into words exactly how he felt.

"You know, just being an outsider in all of this, you didn't have to straddle the guy and repeatedly punch him. That vibe got a little nasty," Archie said.

"Shut up." Vinny sounded pissed.

As far as Gabe was concerned, Vinny didn't have a right to be feeling anything.

"Please, don't fight," Annalise said.

She was the only reason he was staying sane right now. If he'd been left to deal with Vinny on his own, he'd have throttled the little bastard. He couldn't believe Vinny had been so reckless.

He figured Vinny and Annalise were having a good time. Sure, he'd missed her, and wanted her home, but that didn't mean he wanted her to stop having fun.

"Babe, why don't you go and start some dinner for us all? I know I'm starving," Gabe said.

She glanced over at Vinny, biting her lip. For a split second, all Gabe could imagine was those plump lips wrapped around his dick, sucking him down. She would look so pretty on her knees with his cock in her mouth. He'd have to teach her how to suck him just how he liked it.

Damn it.

Annalise messed with his head.

Vinny nodded, and she stood, about to leave the

room, but Gabe couldn't have her doing that. He captured her wrist and pulled her right back against him. "Where's my kiss?"

"You don't seem in the mood to have a kiss."

"When it comes to you, I will always be in the mood." He wasn't angry with Annalise. She'd been scared around those men and the way the creeps had reacted. He got it. If he was completely honest with himself, he wasn't even angry at Vinny. There was no guarantee he wouldn't have reacted in a similar way if he'd been placed in that same position. However, Vinny clearly didn't have all the facts.

Annalise's smile was a big enough distraction for him as she went on her tiptoes, seeing as he was a lot taller than her, and those lips of hers landed right on his.

He cupped her hip with one hand, and with the other, he grabbed the back of her head and deepened the kiss. Gabe wasn't in the mood for sweetness and light. He had this overwhelming need to claim Annalise. To mark her so the world knew he meant business in claiming her.

When he finished, she stepped back. Her lips were slightly reddened as she looked dazed.

"Wow," she said.

He chuckled. "Go ahead."

"Wait a damn minute," Archie said. "I want a kiss too."

Annalise giggled and went over to him, cupping his face, and kissing him. Archie grabbed her around the waist, dragging her down to the sofa and nuzzling her neck.

"Now, I can let you go," Archie said.

Annalise rolled her eyes, and went to Vinny, who stood, stroked her face, and grazed his lips across hers. "I loved today," he whispered.

Gabe couldn't help the twinge of guilt he felt for being such a damn ogre about this. All of them would have reacted to what happened. He couldn't blame Vinny, but clearly, his friend didn't know what was at stake and he needed to let him know.

Sometimes being the oldest sucked.

Annalise left the room, and Vinny turned toward him. "Okay, let me have it. Whatever you've got to say to get shit off your chest, do it!"

"Do you have any idea what you were fucking thinking?" Gabe asked.

"Yeah, they were hassling our woman, so I took care of it. What is the big fucking deal?" Vinny asked.

"The big deal? You don't get it, do you? So I'll spell it out to you. Those men, especially. They work for her fucking stepfather. In case you forgot, he's decided to make things fucking difficult for us." He got the call that very morning, after Vinny had left.

"What do you mean?"

"We've got a few inspectors coming to the ranch, Vinny. That guy you were pummeling also has it in his thick head to press charges on you. So far, the sheriff was able to hold him down. As he said, Annalise had given a statement of harassment, and his inappropriate language, so he talked him down, but this is just the start."

Vinny stopped and looked toward the doorway to where Annalise had left. "That fucker said we'd be sorry. He can't do this, Gabe."

"Well, we've still got an inspection to deal with." Gabe glanced up and down at Vinny. "I told you to be careful. Let's just hope the guy we get isn't in his fucking pocket."

He needed to get some fresh air.

Stepping out of the ranch, he breathed in the warm night air. There were times he hated the heat. The sweat constantly clinging to his back a constant reminder to him of how much work he still needed to get done.

The phone call had pissed him off. Annalise had told them all about the stepfather's inappropriate touching. Now this. It all made complete sense to Gabe. He wouldn't justify the bastard with a name, so he thought of him as stepfucker.

Her stepfucker had been working behind the scenes, manipulating everyone and everything around Annalise, and he finally knew why. He wanted her. This wasn't because she was another man's kid.

Stepfucker wanted Annalise as his own.

It was why he, Vinny, and Archie were a problem.

He couldn't bribe them with money, or anything else, but the ranch. It was their baby, their dream. They'd worked their tears, blood, and sweat into this place, to turn it into a place that finally profited them.

They weren't rolling in dough, but they made enough to get by at the moment. Anything could create a bad turn.

This was so fucked up.

He wasn't going to give up Annalise though. Not for anything. If her stepfucker wanted to play this game, he'd step in the ring. He was used to being without, dealing with assholes willing to take everything from him. He had to wonder just how far stepfucker was going to take this. To Gabe, this life, it was beneath his flesh, written in his core. He knew hardship, pain, loneliness, and downright fucking poverty. He wondered if her stepfather was willing to take that on because Gabe was in this to win it.

****

"Why didn't anyone tell me?" Vinny asked. "A simple phone call would have helped."

Archie sighed. He really didn't want to be dealing with this nightmare. "Seriously? You want to blame us for not getting your ass in the know sooner? Give me a break."

"I didn't know."

"And?" Archie asked.

"If you'd given me the call, I'd have grabbed Annalise and gotten the hell out of there. You know this."

Archie snorted. "What I know is any man who hurts our woman, puts his hands on her, and scares her at all, is going to deal with me. I ain't got a problem with you doing what you did, and let's be honest, Mr. Cool Face out there doesn't have a problem with it. Any other day, we'd all be shaking each other's hands, grabbing an ice-cold beer, and laughing it all off. We don't have that luxury."

"The stepdad did all of this. Why?"

"I'm guessing he's got a hard-on for Annalise. It's the only thing that makes sense."

"I want to kill him." Vinny's hands clenched into fists. They were already cut up from his fight that day.

"Not going to happen. You've done all the pummeling you're allowed to do for the time being. I suggest you go and wash up or do whatever it is you have to do to get your shit together. I'll go and talk to Gabe."

"Since when are you the levelheaded one?" Vinny asked.

"Since you were an asshole and decided to go down a few pegs." Archie stepped out into the night.

When they'd gotten the call from Annalise to go down to the sheriff's office because of what happened, he'd been so pissed.

He'd known about the inspection though, and

knew Gabe was worried. His friend acted like he didn't care, but Archie knew different.

Gabe put himself in the role as their protector, and the truth was, he'd never left it. He put the world on his shoulders, and he hated there was nothing he could do to make this right.

"Hey, big guy," Archie said.

Gabe shook his head. "I'm fine. You don't have to walk on eggshells around me. I'm good."

"I don't know. You seemed pretty pissed in there."

"Nah, not pissed, just dealing with each problem at a time. I took it out on Vinny."

"We both know we would've gutted the guy for touching Annalise," Archie said.

"Oh, I get it. There's no doubt about it. I'm just getting my head together because her stepfucker is going to cause us problems, and we need to be one step ahead."

"I don't see why we would have an issue with this inspection, Gabe. We've already done hundreds of them, even before we opened. We always make sure we're ahead of the game. Those guys always liked to come when we weren't ready. Now they can never find anything wrong."

"We run a tight ship. It's what I'm hoping for."

"What aren't you saying?" Archie asked.

"It's fine."

"Damn it, Gabe. I know you like to play mother hen, but now isn't the time. We're all fully grown men. You don't need to protect us anymore."

"We'll pass the inspection. I have no doubt, but I fear how far he's willing to go. We know those men were sent by him, Archie. It's the start. We can't be all over this ranch. We can't protect all of the cattle, the house, the barns, even our workers at all times."

"You think he's willing to take matters to the next step?"

"I think a man who is desperate for what he wants is willing to do whatever it takes for a specific piece of ass."

"Don't say shit like that."

"Annalise is not a piece of ass to me, Archie. She's our woman, but you've got to be ready for this guy. For what he's going to want."

Archie wanted to tell Gabe that he was overthinking it, expecting the worst-case scenario. The only reason they'd always been one step ahead of the inspections was because of Gabe. He always expected the worst, and oftentimes, he was right.

"Shit." He looked out toward their land, their dream. "I'm not giving her up."

"Wouldn't ask you to. I'm not going to give her up either. She means way too much to me."

"Then what the fuck do we do?" Archie asked.

"We wait and handle every single problem that comes our way, all the while, we need to go after him," Gabe said.

"How? We don't have the kind of money to hire a private investigator." He knew, he'd looked.

After Gabe had taken that phone call, Archie had known they were going to need some help. The cost of a PI was way too much.

"We're going to have to do things our way," Gabe said. "We go backward. We know her landlord was approached and threatened with a similar inspection. So we start to find a path, we further the evidence, and when the time comes, we shut the stepfucker down for good."

"Stepfucker?" Archie asked.

"He doesn't deserve a name."

"I like it. It fits." He nodded, repeating the word

over and over. "You want me to head out and go and talk to the landlord tonight?" The sooner they started this, the quicker it would be over.

"No. He'll be expecting that. We've got to give it a couple of days," Gabe said. "Let me come up with a plan, and we'll handle this our way."

Annalise came to the front door. "Dinner is on the table."

"Woman, you work miracles," Archie said.

She smiled. "Is everything okay here?"

"Peachy," Gabe said, going to her, pulling her in his arms.

"I'm so sorry about what happened."

Gabe pressed a finger to her lips and shook his head. "No, do not apologize for what Vinny did. You were scared, and he protected you. I got no problem with that. You're not allowed off the ranch until I say so, though."

"Wait, what?"

"We're going to protect you, and that, babe, is an order."

Archie didn't like the idea of her stepfather going after her. Not that he could blame the asshole. Annalise was fucking everything, but it also meant if they weren't careful, they were fucked.

****

It didn't take a genius to work out the problem was her stepfather. Annalise felt so guilty. The next day, she shoved her trowel into the soft soil, digging back a hole in order to plant a brand-new bean plant that was ready to go into the ground.

She didn't realize how much she loved gardening until she came to the ranch.

With the five plants of beans dug into the earth, she put the trowel to one side, slowly pushed the soil in, careful not to compact it, and secured the bean.

Vinny had made the frame for the beans to grow up, and it was going to be a big, mighty fine plant.

She got to her feet, went to the water pipe, and filled the two canisters. Lifting them, she walked carefully across to the beans and gave them a good watering.

In a couple of weeks, or months, they would have some fresh beans for meals. Just the thought of turning a bunch of them into a spicy stew made her mouth water.

Until then, she had to harvest what was available. She went into the small greenhouse and saw an abundance of ripe tomatoes. The basket was on the counter, and she began to hum as she picked each beautiful fruit. Annalise never wasted a thing, but modified her menu based on what was available.

Her men weren't big on salads, but she was in the mood for something light and fresh.

She had a nice hot chili in the oven. Super spicy. All she needed to do was finish off the cornbread batter, and of course grill up some corn when the time was right.

After the tomatoes, she went to the herb garden. It would all need washing. She picked a selection, then gave everything a good wash, feeling the heat of the sun blaring down on the back of her neck.

Gabe had taken his time this morning to apply plenty of sunscreen to her body. Being a natural redhead, she also had pale skin that burned easily. He'd told her he didn't want her to get sunstroke, which was why she wore the large straw hat.

She loved how they cared. It felt good to matter to someone.

After living for so long with people who liked to pretend she didn't exist, their attention meant the world to her.

He's going to take it all away.

Annalise paused, holding her bounty and feeling a wave of fear run down her spine at the very thought.

Her stepfather had taken so much from her, and she knew he was intent on destroying Gabe, Vinny, and Archie. The man was a control freak who always had to win. She wouldn't let that happen. There was no way he could get away with this.

He was a monster.

She stepped into the house and gasped as she was suddenly picked up and pressed against the kitchen table.

At first, she thought her stepfather was there, but as Archie's scent surrounded her, she calmed her pounding heart and smiled up at him.

"Archie, you scared me."

He spread her legs open, and then she felt exactly how excited he was to see her.

She arched up, gasping.

The skirt she wore didn't hide anything, and as he pressed his face against her neck, his palm went between her thighs, touching her.

"Are you wet for me?" he asked.

She hadn't been aroused, but his touch, his scent, that was all she needed. It pushed all of her bad thoughts out of her mind, and she was totally focused on the now with Archie.

That evil bastard from her past was not going to spoil another moment of her life. She wouldn't let him, not for a second.

Archie slid his fingers beneath her skirt, stroking over her clit, and she cried out.

"Oh, fuck, you're so wet, baby. I've struggled to do any kind of work, thinking about this." He slid his tongue across her neck, biting down on her pulse, and she whimpered. His finger traced across her clit, once, twice, a third time, before sliding down, going to her entrance.

He circled her opening, and then slowly with the tip of his finger, he pushed inside her.

Annalise whimpered.

"You're so fucking tight."

He pushed his finger deeper inside her, and she sank her teeth into her lip, trying to hold in a gasp.

Archie set her on fire. All three of her men did. All it took was a single touch, or even a kiss, and she was ready for them.

She sat up on the table and placed her hand on his chest, feeling the rush of his heart. Nerves threatened to take over, but she ignored them as she traced her hand down his body, going toward his pants.

The hardness of his length surprised her.

"Yeah, baby, touch me."

She loved the sounds he made.

He stepped away, and she watched as he worked over the front of his jeans and slid his zipper down, being careful as he brushed it over his dick.

Licking her lips, she waited and then moaned as the fullness of him was exposed to her view.

The tip was already wet with his pre-cum, and he worked his fist up and down the length. His entire body was hard and ripped with muscle. She couldn't believe this was the same man who'd been bullied as a child for being a runt.

"Do you like what you see?"

She nodded.

Climbing off the table, she went to her knees before him.

"Oh, fuck."

"I want to taste you, Archie." She put her hands on his, matching each of his strokes in time. "Will you show me?"

"Yeah, fuck, yes."

She couldn't resist licking the tip and letting out a moan at the taste of him.

"Now that's a pretty sight," Vinny said.

Annalise didn't look toward the new voice. She was too lost in her own lust, covering Archie's dick with her lips and slowly sucking him into her mouth. She loved the feel of him as he slid inside.

Another groan, this time coming from Gabe, and she opened her eyes, not realizing that she'd closed them. All three of her men looked down at her with wonder in their eyes.

It was oddly titillating having the other men watch their intimate moment. A mix of a deep connection and dirty that she couldn't get enough of.

She bobbed her head over Archie's cock, over and over, focusing on this thick shaft and not worrying if she was doing it right or not. By the sounds he made, she knew he was enjoying it. His fingers tightened in her hair, making her eyes water. She kept going, taking him deeper, faster, until he gripped her head with both hands and groaned as jets of his cum hit the back of her throat.

After he pulled away, falling back into an armchair, Gabe took his place, his huge cock bouncing in front of her face. She didn't hesitate, covering him with her mouth, tasting his salty pre-cum.

"Fuck yeah."

She gave Gabe the same attention, fucking him thoroughly with her mouth, sucking and taking him deep. The only difference was the fact he pulled away before coming into her mouth. She felt incomplete, craving more, opening her eyes to see what was wrong.

He was pumping his cock in his fist as Vinny unzipped in front of her.

"Give me a little of that, okay, baby girl?"

She nodded, her lips swollen with lust. Annalise suckled Vinny's big, hard erection while Gabe pumped his dick less than a foot away. This time, she kept her eyes open to watch.

Archie got up and moved behind her, unbuttoning her blouse until it fell to her waist. Her breasts were bare, bouncing slightly as she slid up and down Vinny's length. Archie played with her nipples, kissing her back.

Then he moved away briskly. Vinny pulled away from her mouth and joined Gabe in coming all over her tits. It was filthy and perfect.

"Tonight will be all about you, sweetheart."

Chapter Ten

She had a few days to prepare everything for Gabe's surprise birthday party. Forty-five was a big deal, even if he wanted to let it go by without notice. Annalise had all the ingredients for the cake, balloons, candles, and enough food to feed an army. She planned to make all his favorites. What she needed was the perfect gift.

The men were busy in the fields. Vinny was going to take her shopping in the evening, but she had no clue what to look for. Gabe was an enigma. He didn't really have any hobbies or interests besides working day and night. Since she moved in, she ascertained that he loved animals, especially the dogs. But that still didn't help her choose a gift.

It was driving her crazy.

She wanted him to feel special, to know how much he meant to her. But her mind was still a blank.

Gabe didn't like celebrating his birthday, but she wouldn't let such a special day pass by without notice. That went for all of the men.

Her phone rang. As soon as she heard his voice, her blood turned to ice. She was transported back in time, once again a vulnerable girl in the sites of a predator.

"How did you get this number?"

"You of all people should know I always have my ways," Raymond said.

"What do you want?"

He laughed, the sound making a shiver run up her spine. "I'm sending a car over. It will be at the ranch in fifteen minutes. Get inside and don't ask questions."

"Why would I do that?"

"Annalise, are you willing to ruin three lives? One call and their entire operation could be closed down permanently."

"Why would you do that? They've done nothing to you."

"You have a lot of questions. They're just collateral damage to get what I want. Now, follow my directions and you won't have to worry about it, will you? From what I've seen, you haven't thrived without me. You won't miss some odd waitressing jobs, I assure you."

He hung up on her before she could ask the million other questions she needed to ask. What did he want from her? Where was he taking her?

They'd been in hot water ever since Vinny got into a fight with the inspectors. They were sent by her stepfather, the first sign that he was ready to take this all the way. He wanted her to do his bidding and wouldn't take no for an answer.

After high school, she'd left home. Life had been hell since her mother remarried, and even though she'd been promised financial support, she refused it all in favor of her freedom. She was happier in her shitty apartment and minimum-wage job at the diner than living like a prisoner. The last couple of years before she left, her stepfather had become more handsy. She'd tried to tell her mother, but her only response was that Annalise was luring him, acting inappropriately. None of it was true, but it still hurt that her mother would defend that man rather than believe her.

She felt alone, victimized, and desperate.

It got to the point that Annalise was scared of her own shadow. He'd be waiting for her around corners, trying to get her alone to press his body against hers and push the boundaries more and more. Her escape had been a long time coming, and she never looked back.

Now that pig was trying to weasel his way back into her life. For what?

Annalise couldn't take any risks when it came to Gabe, Vinny, and Archie. She loved and cared about them too much for them to get hurt. No way would she let her dysfunctional family drama ruin everything they'd built together. They were hardworking cowboys she respected. They didn't deserve Raymond's wrath. She knew what it felt like to be on the receiving end.

The car pulled up to the front of the house exactly fifteen minutes later. Her cowboys would be out in the fields until dinner, so there was no way they knew what was going on at the house. Annalise always looked forward to preparing their meal. They were always so grateful and ate everything she served.

She stepped outside into the heat, the screen door slapping shut behind her. For a couple of minutes, she just stood here, indecision making her crazy. But she couldn't back down now. Couldn't be selfish. She got into the back of the car, only a driver inside.

"Where are you taking me?"

"Mr. Davenport's office."

She hated that name. As soon as she had enough money, she was changing her last name. It didn't belong to her, not really, and she wanted no part of it.

There was no point in talking or asking the driver questions. She leaned back and watched the trees flash by her window. It was a long drive to the city, the landscape transforming until they were surrounded by skyscrapers. She hadn't been back to the city for years and didn't miss it at all.

They stopped at a garage door, then drove down the winding drive until they arrived at the underground elevators. The lighting was dim, the scent of gasoline strong. Someone else was there to escort her up to his office. It felt like a prisoner transfer, and in a way, it was.

She hadn't said one word the entire trip, even

now as she allowed them to usher her here and there, until Annalise finally stood in front of his office door.

"How was your trip?" Raymond asked upon opening the door.

"Why am I here?"

He only chuckled and waved a hand for her to enter. Every nerve in her body was a livewire. She didn't know what to expect from him.

After closing the door behind her, he pointed to an empty chair in front of his desk. "I'm glad you came."

"I didn't have much choice," she said.

"Well, I have a proposition for you, one you can't refuse." He flashed that evil smile. The man was a sociopath. "I want you to work for me. Here. I'll arrange an apartment for you in the building. Very convenient, no?"

"No."

"Annalise. Annalise. You never should have run off like you did."

"You never treated me like a daughter. Every day in that house I lived in fear. I had no choice but to leave."

"You're not my daughter though, are you? A daughter wouldn't give me a daily hard-on. And you were just begging for my attention, weren't you?"

"No!" She bolted out of her seat and stood behind it. "What does my mother think of this proposition?"

He shrugged. "As long as her credit card has no limit, she doesn't give a shit what I do with my free time."

Tears pricked her eyes, but she forced them away. She was too angry to feel hurt or betrayed. That ship had sailed before she left home.

"Well, I'm not for sale. I don't want your job or your apartment. I'm an adult, not a child to toy with. What don't you understand about that?"

"I will have you one way or another. Do you realize how many people are on my payroll? How many branches of government react when I snap my fingers?"

"Why? Why me?"

"You're the little fish that got away."

He was obsessed, determined to have her in his bed. The mere thought made her sick to the stomach. She didn't want him to get one finger on her, but at the same time, she knew what he was capable of. Her plan to rat him out to her mother came crumbling apart when she realized now, more than ever, her mother didn't love her. She had her new, luxurious life and that didn't include Annalise. Surely someone would disapprove of his deranged idea. Was there anyone out there left to defend her?

****

Vinny saw the tracks leaving the property. There had been a car there at some point today, he was certain of it.

With everything going on with the inspectors and the law lately, it wasn't a good sign.

"Annalise?"

He ran up the stairs, checking all the bedrooms. There was no sign of her inside or out in the barns. No note. Nothing.

She'd been busy planning Gabe's birthday party in private lately, but he'd promised to take her shopping after supper. It didn't make sense for her to call a taxi and not wait for him. She'd been so excited about their plans.

He called Annalise's cell phone. She only took the old thing along if she left the ranch. Gabe and Archie plodded into the house, kicking off their boots and hanging up their hats. It has been a long, hot, grueling day.

"Baby, I'm starving."

He tried to ignore his friends' voices.

Someone answered the cell phone, but all he heard were sobs.

"Annalise?"

More crying and a few attempts to speak. It had to be her. Where the hell was she? What happened?

"Are you okay, Annalise? Answer me, woman!"

"What's going on? Where's Annalise?" Gabe asked, coming closer.

Vinny waved him away so he could hear on the phone.

"I don't know what to do," she said. "I'm in the city at my stepfather's office. He wants to force me to stay here. If I don't, he'll make life hell for you as payback. I feel so trapped and scared, but I can't just walk away."

"How'd you get there?"

"He sent someone to pick me up. I had no choice, Vinny. I swear. I'm thirty years old, and I still can't control my own life."

"You sure can. Send me the address. I'll come and get you straight away."

"He'll shut you down. No, worse. His revenge has no limits," she said.

He heard the fear in her voice and knew firsthand that it wasn't unfounded. She was right. Raymond Davenport could make their lives miserable. Years of hard work and struggling would all be for nothing.

"We'll find a way. I'm getting you back. I won't stop until I do."

She began to sob again. The hopelessness of their situation was getting the best of her. Even now, he tried to think of every scenario that could leave them on top. None came to mind. He needed to inspire her, to give her hope.

"I've got to go," she said. "I hear someone coming."

She hung up the phone before he could respond.

"Annalise? Annalise!"

Vinny crashed down on the sofa with a groan, the phone still in his hand.

"What's going on?" Gabe asked. "Tell me now."

He took a breath. "Her stepfather showed up. He's forcing her to stay in the city. She called from his office in tears. That bastard is planning to keep her for himself."

"He's keeping her as some kind of concubine," Archie said. "What a freak."

"Well, let's go get her. The sooner we start the drive, the sooner we'll be back to take care of the ranch," Gabe said.

Vinny shook his head. "You understand what we're dealing with more than anyone. Don't you remember giving me slack for fighting with those inspectors? You went on and on about how I could have ruined everything for us. Her stepfather has power, money, and connections. He'll shut us down and have us tied up in so much litigation, we'll be miserable."

"So we just forget about her?" Archie said, pacing back and forth in front of them. "Forget she never came into our lives and find ourselves another woman to share that's more convenient?"

"Never said that." Vinny rubbed his temples. "We just have to think on this. Do it the right way."

"He's got a wife, doesn't he?" Gabe said. "I'm sure she'll put a stop to all this once she finds out. I mean, the man wants to fuck his own stepdaughter."

"She's got serious mommy issues, so don't count on that plan working out," Vinny said. "We're all she has in the world."

He needed to get some air. His emotions were getting the better of him.

Vinny left the house, heading to the barn. The dogs followed him, but he wasn't in a playful mood. He knew they were wondering where Annalise was. She usually gave them leftovers from cooking dinner about now.

The house felt so empty without her. She was the heart of the home.

He'd been drifting through life, trying to look on the positive side. But since Annalise showed up in their lives, he'd finally realized what was missing. He needed the security and connection of a serious relationship, a forever love. A woman to share. She was unique, a perfect fit for the three of them. It was like all the hardships had led them all together.

Now this.

Vinny had to come up with a way to get Annalise back without jeopardizing everything. They didn't have six figures in the bank or friends in high places. They were lowly working men, easily crushed by sharks like Raymond Davenport.

"You were ready to knock those assholes into next week for her. Now you're scared to make a move," Archie said.

"Fuck you."

"Maybe you're not good enough for her."

He whirled around on his friend. Why couldn't he have stayed in the house and given him some damn breathing room? "Listen, you have no idea how much I need her, how much I want her. It's killing me on the inside. But who the hell am I to take on a man like Davenport?"

"Then I'll go on my own. I'm ready to go to hell

for that woman," Archie said.

"Don't claim you care more than me. You don't."

****

"Pass me a bottle of water," said Gabe.

He'd been driving for hours, and the GPS said they were only ten minutes away from the Davenport towers. There had never been a reason to drive this far south. The noise, traffic, and concrete jungle surrounding their old pick-up truck were unnerving.

"Stop there," Vinny said, pointing to a coffee shop at the corner.

Since Annalise had no clue they'd driven all the way here to rescue her, and they weren't sure exactly where she was, they needed to regroup.

"Good evening, cowboys." The waitress giggled after they entered the shop. It was past dinner hour, so the place wasn't too busy.

"Can we get a table for the three of us?" Gabe asked.

"Sure thing. Follow me."

Their waitress was busy flirting while everyone else in the place focused on staring. Were they that out of place in the city? It didn't make sense. He was only wearing blue jeans, a navy t-shirt, and a plaid padded coat. Was it the boots? The hat?

"Something wrong with the way we're dressed?" he asked the waitress once they were seated.

She smiled and twirled a lock of her hair around a finger. "You're just very big boys." She winked. "We usually get suits in here, not cowboys."

They ordered coffee and began to talk about their next move.

"You should call her again," Gabe said. "Get an update from her."

"What if she wants to stay? What if his offer was

too good to refuse?" Archie asked.

"Are you fucking dumb?" Vinny asked. "She was crying her heart out. No way does she want to be here."

"We'll lose the ranch."

Archie and Vinny quieted once he spoke.

It was a fact, a sobering one, but they'd all agreed Annalise was worth it. Even if they had to live in a rented shack, as long as they had each other, they'd get by.

"Well, who could help us? I mean, there must be places that help the small guys. What if we go to the local news station with the truth?"

"Archie, I doubt a news station would want to go against Davenport," Gabe said. "I wouldn't be surprised if his company was a sponsor."

"What if he had a tragic accident in the parking lot after work?" Vinny asked.

"Just stop," Gabe said. "Call Annalise. We're getting nowhere fast."

He sipped on his coffee as Vinny made the call. His stomach was in knots with so many unknowns. He thrived on routine and security. This whole adventure was completely out of his comfort zone.

"How's everything going?" Vinny asked after Annalise answered. He listened for a long stretch. "Tell me where you're staying exactly. We're coming to get you." Another quiet spell.

Gabe had no clue what Annalise was saying yet. The suspense was killing him.

"We right around the corner, so there's no backing out now, baby girl," Vinny said. "Yeah. Okay. We can do that."

After telling her how much he loved her, Vinny hung up the phone.

"Well?" Archie said.

"She's real surprised we're here. No one's ever

done anything like this for her."

"And?"

"Tomorrow morning at nine thirty, she wants us to come and meet with her stepfather, give him our best case and see what he says."

Gabe frowned. "That doesn't seem right. She knows he won't bend."

"Well, maybe she's desperate and hoping for a miracle. All I know is we can't say no to her request."

"We'll be there. It'll take every bit of willpower not to punch that stepfucker right in the face," Gabe said.

"If the level-headed one is resorting to violence, we're all doomed." Vinny laughed.

Their situation was so fucked up it really was laughable. He'd never begged for anything in his life, and now he had to bow down to that piece-of-shit Davenport so he wouldn't force Annalise to be his sex slave. How had this happened?

"We'll have to get a room for the night," Gabe said. "It's getting late. Call the ranch hands and tell them we won't be there in the morning."

God willing, all four of them would be home enjoying one of Annalise's dinners tomorrow. They'd laugh about all this bullshit and move on with the rest of their lives. But deep down, he wasn't so certain of anything anymore.

Chapter Eleven

Archie didn't like this. Everything in his body screamed for him to get as far away from all of this shit as possible, but he couldn't leave without Annalise.

None of them had talked that morning. Each of them going through the motions as if their lives weren't in the hands of an evil fucker.

Vinny looked ready to murder, while Gabe had been quieter than usual, which was really strange, seeing as he already wasn't much of a talker. As for himself, he'd spent most of the night tossing and turning, waiting for the right answers to come and take him.

Nothing helped.

He didn't know how to go up against a man with money and everyone in his pocket.

They arrived at a café in the city near their hotel. This one was so busy, and none of them stood out as they ordered some breakfast.

Archie sat at their table, sipping his hot coffee but not really tasting it. There was nothing to enjoy right now.

Everything rested in the hands of an obsessive man.

"You know, I was thinking," Vinny said.

He turned toward his friend.

"Annalise has been on her own ever since she got out. She doesn't strike me as a woman who would try to face this shit on her own. That means she told her mother, and the old bat didn't do anything," Vinny said.

"That's a pretty big leap," Gabe said.

"Do you see her calling her mother?" Archie asked. He'd already figured out that Annalise had tried to tell her mother what was happening and wasn't heard. No one would just go straight to running away from their problems unless no one was willing to help. "She has no one."

Gabe shook his head. "What kind of woman doesn't believe their daughter? We're jumping to conclusions."

Archie shook his head and took another sip of the rancid coffee. Considering the price, he expected it to be like liquid gold or something. It was disgusting. He'd much rather be waking up with Annalise in his bed and waiting for her coffee to finish brewing.

He missed her so damn much.

"You know he's not going to agree to us taking her," Gabe said.

"I know." This came from Vinny.

"It's not going to stop us from trying," Archie said.

Gabe sighed. "You know, I thought all women were the fucking same. They were only interested in causing trouble. I was happy to live alone, to not give any thought to what I was missing out on. Until you guys brought a new housekeeper home and nothing was ever the same."

"Annalise has helped us all see what we were missing," Archie said.

"We're not giving her up. We're going to win this," Vinny said. "One way or another."

He couldn't see Vinny's hands, but he would bet his life savings the guy had his fists clenched. Out of all of them, he had a feeling Vinny would be the one who would put a person into an early grave. If it wasn't for Gabe, the guy wouldn't have any kind of control.

Finishing his coffee, he checked the time on the clock above the café's counter.

They still had two hours to get to the meeting.

None of them ordered any food but drank their

weight in coffee.

"I miss her," Gabe said. "We can't give her a good life."

Archie rolled his eyes. "Are we seriously going to do this?"

"Look around you. We all know that her stepfather has money. He has the means of giving her a good life. The perfect life."

Vinny shook his head. "You're willing to give her to a pervert? That's what he is. He was supposed to see her as a daughter. Who'd want to hook up with a thing like that?"

"They're not related by blood," Gabe said. "What life can we offer her? Hard work? Lots of kids to run after? Struggling from one year to the next?"

Archie burst out laughing. "Wow, you must really have your head up your ass. Annalise doesn't want material things, Gabe. She wants the one thing that she's been denied all her life. Our woman, and that is exactly what she is, wants love. Is that so hard for you to figure out?"

"I do love her."

"Then focus on that. We're not going to be destroying Annalise's life. We're going to be giving her the life she always wanted. We're three men who love her, her and only her. She is the only woman I want in my bed, bearing my children. I see a life with her, a future, and I'm not allowing some fucker to take that from me. Annalise is ours, so stop doing that shit. You did it while we were growing up, worried that you were hurting us in some way." He got it. Gabe took all the responsibility on his shoulders, even when he didn't need to.

He and Vinny had been there for Gabe. No one had wanted this gruff man, but they sure did.

Archie got to his feet. The air in the café was far too thin.

"Where're you going?" Gabe asked.

He pulled out several bills and put them on the table. "I need some air. I'm stepping out for a few minutes." He didn't give Gabe time to moan at him. He stepped out of the café into the horrible city air.

Nothing was clean here. And he could only see as far as across the street.

Life at the ranch had always been hard, but he preferred it to this.

This life wasn't fun. Sure, ranch work was hard, painful, and tiring, but he loved it. He wouldn't change it for anything else, and he certainly wasn't going to let Annalise live a life of luxury that she clearly didn't want. Or was he being selfish? Did Annalise want that life?

Memories of her sweet smile as she worked at the ranch, cooking, gardening, helping them with the animals assailed him. She had loved every minute of it. He couldn't imagine her wanting anything else. Whatever happened, it would be Annalise's decision. He'd never felt this close to fucking losing it, but his very future was hanging in the balance.

****

"Have you come to your senses?" Raymond asked.

Annalise felt sick as he grabbed her shoulders and gave them a gentle massage from behind. His touch repulsed her. Everything about this man disgusted her.

He hated the word *no*, but that was all she had to offer.

She was lucky to have gotten away from him for as long as she did, but now, she was back within his trap.

Vinny said they were coming for her. She'd lied and hadn't told Raymond they were on their way. The hope was that her stepfather would be so surprised it would fool him into saying the stuff she needed him to say. She was done with him. This had to end.

Raymond wasn't going to get away with this, and there was no way she was going to give in to him, not now, not ever.

His hands started to move down toward her chest, but she jerked up out of her seat and spun around to face him. He burst out laughing and her body shook.

"You never stop, do you?" he asked.

"When are you going to realize I don't want this? I don't want you."

"Oh, please, women are all the same. They love to manipulate men, and you're no different. Why do you keep on fighting me? You will want for nothing. All you have to do is give me what I want."

"Stop!" She yelled the word. "Just stop! There is nothing I want from you." She shoved her hands in her pockets and clicked the button on her cell phone. Her hands shook but with his touch, he wouldn't have the first clue as to what she was doing. She only hoped that she had done the right thing. "You're my stepfather, Raymond Davenport!"

"So? What has my name got to do with anything? You and I both know I can have whatever the hell I want, and you, Annalise, have been mine since the moment I put a ring on your mother's finger." He shook his head and rounded his office desk. "I thought a night in the apartment I've got planned for you would put a stop to this nonsense."

She laughed. "You think one night in a fancy apartment would seal the deal for me to become your mistress?"

"Yes. You have always been mine, Annalise. Do you really think I married that old cunt for any other reason other than you?"

This made Annalise pause. Every time she had seen Raymond and her mother together, they always looked happy. She felt like a child looking in from the window, unwanted and cast off.

"What?"

"Does it surprise you, darling, to know that all along I intended to take her daughter? You see, Annalise, you were a beautiful young girl, but that isn't the way I swing." He shuddered. "I knew if I waited for you, you were going to be a beautifully delicious woman." His gaze traveled down her body. "And believe me when I say this, I was right." His hands ran down his chest all the way to his cock, and she watched as he squeezed himself.

She was so close to throwing up.

"Do you have any idea how often I've imagined fucking you?" he asked. "Thinking of you riding my cock, taking it deep into your mouth. Turn around."

"What?"

"You heard me. Turn around."

Annalise felt tears fill her eyes, but she turned, presenting him with her back.

"And I'm going to fuck that ass as well. I imagine those cowboys have done a good job of breaking you in. At first, I was so pissed off. That cherry was supposed to be mine to pop, but now, I don't have to worry about damaging you. You'll be ready to be fucked hard."

Each word out of his mouth made her anxiety rise. "You're a monster."

"Am I though, really?"

"You've manipulated my life. You've forced me out of work. You have taken everything from me, to what? Own me?" She shook her head. "You're not fair."

"Newsflash, darling. Life isn't fair. In this world,

you have to play dirty to get what you want, and guess what, I am going to get you." He reached into his drawer. "You think I wouldn't challenge those assholes if I didn't know every single little detail about them?" He pulled out a manila file folder.

He slapped it on his desk, opened it up, and flicked through the pages. Annalise had no choice but to step a little closer, and then she saw what it was. A file on her men. Gabe. Archie. Vinny.

"Do you have any idea how hard those men have worked? How close they've come to losing everything?" He tutted as he flicked through page after page of details. "The loans they borrowed. The amount they had to pay back. All the years of hard work, and it could go in an instant. They really beat the odds, you know. It's almost admirable."

"Don't," she said.

"Don't what?"

"Don't hurt them." She couldn't bear the thought of her men suffering because of her.

"We'll see if they allow me to leave them alone," Raymond said.

"What do you mean?"

"You think I don't know that you contacted them? I had eyes on them. They're heading right this way." He leaned back in his chair, putting his hands behind his head. Raymond smiled that evil grin. "What's the matter, Annalise? Are you going to admit defeat?"

"Never," she said. "Do you really think you're going to enjoy forcing me?"

"But that is the beauty of all of this, Annalise. It's not going to be force, and you want to know why? You're going to come to my bed, willing and begging me to take you, because if you don't, I'll make sure your men pay."

His torture wouldn't end.

Annalise wanted to yell at him, but instead, she held her tongue as his office door was banged open.

She glanced behind her, seeing Gabe, Vinny, and Archie stepping into her stepfather's office.

There was no way she could risk them losing anything. Her cell phone was still turned on. Now it was her time to play dirty and to finally get rid of her stepfather once and for all.

****

Vinny was being a good boy.

Staring across the room at Raymond Davenport, all he wanted to do was charge at him, to unleash his fists. Instead, he held himself firm.

Losing his shit right now wouldn't be in any of their best interests, even though he couldn't deny it would give him immeasurably pleasure to wipe that smug smile off the bastard's face.

One look at Annalise, and he knew they were making the right decision. She didn't want to belong to her stepfather. This life in the city didn't suit her. They weren't making a big mistake.

"Well, well, well, if it's not her loyal protectors. I thought you boys would be getting your ranch up to standard. Never had an inspector see such sloppy work."

"Cut the crap," Gabe said. "You know why we're here."

"Oh, believe me, I don't. Annalise lied to you. She didn't arrange for a meeting. She tried to get you here to surprise me, and I guess it worked, I'm surprised. Anyone who has tried to help Annalise in the past has always been easily bought off, but you boys, you're proving to be a real pain in my ass." He held up a file. "You see this? This is every single detail of your life. You boys have worked hard for everything you got, so why don't we settle this like men. I can make all your troubles go away. All you've got to do is leave Annalise to me." Raymond looked at each of them in turn and chuckled. "I mean, it's not like you boys can offer her a better life. Look at you. I'm surprised you kept that shit hole open for as long as you have." He flicked open the file. "And you're all turning a profit now. But you're no match for me."

"You have no idea what they built," Annalise said.

"I know exactly what they built, and it would be so easy to tear it down."

"How did you do it?" Annalise asked.

"Excuse me?" Raymond asked.

Vinny frowned as he looked at Annalise. She turned her back on them and swung her hips as she walked toward Raymond. She put her hands flat on his desk, leaning forward, her big tits nearly in his face.

He didn't get it.

She hated her stepfather, but the way she walked wasn't in sync. Everything about her screamed attraction. The additional sway of her hips, how she leaned over, almost tempting.

"Tell me how you want to win me over."

Raymond smiled and stood. "Is that what you want?"

"Yeah, I need to know exactly how far you're willing to go to get me. My mother didn't want me, but the lifestyle you provided. No one has ever wanted me for me, and let's be frank, the only thing those boys want is their ranch, so tell me, Raymond, what is it you want? You're right. I'm tired of fighting you. I'm tired of everything. You always win, but the least you can do is tell me how you do it."

"Now that's a beautiful sight. You see, Annalise,

I know that by helping people, they have to owe me a favor. The inspector I sent to you, he has a little drug problem, and so all I had to do was give him the supply he needed, and then he was able to butcher the ranch as he walked around. It's so easy. Everyone is always so busy that a little tug here, a snap there, and safety is so important you know."

"It sounds easy enough," she said.

Vinny had to stand and listen as Raymond bragged with pride about every single demeaning thing he'd done in the last several years in his attempt to finally push Annalise into a desperate corner.

He wanted his stepdaughter begging for his help so he would have all the power.

"Now, I've got you."

There was a pause.

"No, you don't," Annalise said. "You disgust me, you vile creature." The sudden turn of Annalise startled Vinny as she stepped away from the desk. She kept on walking away. "This ends today. You are not going to hurt these men. You're going to leave their ranch alone, and you will leave me alone."

Raymond frowned. "That's not happening."

Vinny watched as Annalise pulled her cell phone from her pocket. She clicked a button, and the sound of Raymond's voice filled the room.

"You little bitch."

"It was time for me to take a leaf out of your book, Raymond. You said so yourself, you get everything you want by playing dirty. You thought I wanted them here to try to convince you to leave me alone. It wasn't. I knew you wouldn't be able to resist telling me the details of how you ruined my life. That's why I didn't tell you, and you fell for it. I hate you. You disgust me."

"You're not going to get away with this."

"Yeah, I am, because if you don't leave me alone, and if I find out that you did this to any other woman, I will take this to the cops. Maybe the media."

Vinny had heard enough. "Fuck this. You're finished, Raymond. Good luck," he said, grabbing Annalise's arm. Without another look, he took her away from her stepfather and out of the city that he was pretty sure was giving him hives.

Chapter Twelve

"Blow out the candles," Annalise chanted.

Gabe was being difficult, but she could see the little smile pulling at the corners of his mouth. He was pure sex appeal, ruggedly handsome and brooding.

"Come on, we don't have all day," Vinny said.

"Okay. Okay." Gabe moved in closer to the cake she'd made. Annalise had put all her love into it, even finding out Gabe's favorite flavors and fruits to make it perfect.

"Don't forget to make a wish," she said just before he blew out all the candles.

He stopped briefly and winked at her. How could such a simple act make her heart beat faster? She was in love.

Gabe blew out the candles, then stood back upright. She hugged his side, and he tucked her in close. "What did you wish for?" she asked.

"Can't tell you that."

"I don't know if I can eat a piece of cake after that meal," Archie said. He sat in the recliner with the required birthday hat on his head.

"It's strawberry shortcake," Vinny said.

Archie shrugged. "I guess I'll find room then."

She began to slice the cake, placing pieces on the cute disposable plates she'd bought weeks ago for today. Annalise couldn't help but wonder if her men had any happy childhood birthday memories. They'd had hard lives growing up, but that was the past now.

After a few hours of relaxing in the living room, allowing their food to digest, they all headed outside for a bonfire.

Gabe and Archie gathered the kindling and logs while Vinny got the fire started. She sat back on one of the log benches with a warm shawl around her shoulders. Although the days were scorching hot, the evenings had a nip to them.

"Did you see the look on his face?" Archie said.

"It was pretty rewarding," Gabe said, dropping an armful of cut wood from the pile they kept by the barn. They heated the house with wood in the winter months, and they were always prepared well in advance.

"At least we don't have to worry about overzealous inspectors again." Vinny got the fire roaring. She could already feel the heat, the sparks flying up into the dark night sky. Out here in the country, they could really enjoy the stars. This was exactly where she wanted to be. She wouldn't trade all the luxuries in the world for the simple life.

"I didn't think we'd be able to get out of that mess," Gabe said, sitting down next to her on the bench. He set a strong hand on her thigh.

"Thanks to Annalise, we'll never have to worry about him again," Archie said.

It was true that things felt hopeless for a while. She would have sacrificed her own happiness to save the ranch and ensure her cowboys weren't put through hell because of her stepfather. But now she could breathe. With the recording in her possession, he'd move on and leave them all alone.

She didn't need her so-called family because she had her own.

Annalise turned to Gabe. The evening was perfect, the sounds of nature all around them. "I'm sorry, but I didn't get you a gift. I wanted to, but I couldn't think of anything."

He kissed her forehead. "I don't need a present from you. You made an amazing dinner and birthday. Most of all you cared, you tried to make my day special.

That means a lot."

"Did I succeed?"

"Best birthday ever," he said.

"Oh, I know a way or two it can be even better," Vinny said. The other two cowboys were sitting opposite them now, the dancing flames between them.

"Such as?" she asked.

Vinny ran a hand through his hair. "I don't know. You naked. The three of us sharing you."

"It's my birthday, not yours," Gabe said.

"Don't be cruel," Archie said. "We did your work all day. It wasn't a cake walk."

"True."

Gabe had taken the entire day off. The guys insisted on it. He'd relaxed in the hammock while she cooked. Of course, she made sure to bring him fresh lemonade and wait on him every chance she got.

"That's a good idea," she said. "Anything Gabe wants since I didn't buy a gift."

They all chuckled.

"What?" she asked.

"Careful what you wish for, baby girl," Gabe said.

Annalise knew precisely what they wanted, and she was more than ready. Their unique ménage relationship wouldn't feel complete until they filled her at the same time, binding them, making this symbolically official. Just thinking about it made her pussy weep and clench. Their bodies were hard with muscle, rugged, and scarred. One cock would be deep in her cunt, satisfying the deep-seated ache. Another would be in her mouth. The third would take her virgin ass, stretching her, making her impossibly full of cowboy cock.

They were filthy but loving. Virile but patient and attentive. She felt safe with each one of them, trusted them, and wanted to spend the rest of her life with all three of them.

The way they looked at her drove her crazy with desire. They made her feel beautiful, sexy, and wanted. She couldn't believe how lucky she'd become after such a rocky start in her life. Tonight was about Gabe though, making his birthday sex more than memorable. She'd trust him with her body because she'd already given him her heart.

****

Gabe never thought he'd see this day at his age, but there was no denying it—he was completely head over heels in love with Annalise. She was a mix of innocence and determination. As she watched the fireflies with magical wonder, he knew he'd do anything for her. She was the complete opposite from the women he'd dated in the past.

Right now, all he wanted to do was spread her thighs and claim her over and over again. They'd all enjoyed sharing her and sometimes she'd sleep with only one of them at a time. It worked for them. They'd never shared her in the traditional sense, fucking her at the same time. It had been a fantasy on his mind since their first night together.

No way Archie and Vinny hadn't thought about it too. It was a balancing act to not scare her away and move to that next step in their ménage relationship.

"We should head inside. It's getting cold," he said.

She nodded, hugging her shawl tighter.

Vinny handled dousing the fire as Gabe led Annalise inside.

"You liked your birthday?" she asked.

"I loved my birthday." He checked his watch. "It's not quite over yet, is it?"

She smiled.

Once they were all inside, all eyes were on her. She set her shawl on the back of the sofa and flicked her red hair back.

"Maybe we should do this here for a change," she said.

He watched her slip out of her pants and tug off her sweater. She stood there in the dimly lit room in just her bra and panties.

"Look at that body," Vinny said. "Does it belong to us?"

"You know it does," she said. "It's never belonged to anyone else, and certainly not my stepfather."

"Let's not talk about him," Archie said, motioning her to take off more with a wave of his hand.

Gabe felt his cock stirring as she slid the first strap of her bra down. She was being a tease, moving slowly, seductively. She was usually more shy than risqué. He wasn't complaining.

"All the way off," Vinny said.

Her bra fell to the floor, her big, lush tits on public display. His mouth salivated with the desire to suck on her firm pink nipples.

"You may as well go all the way, baby." Archie leaned over his knees, watching intently.

She didn't say a word, shimmying out of her panties until she stood in the living room completely naked. Her soft, pale skin and every rounded curve were things of beauty. Her breasts sloped out into tempting peaks, her hips round and inviting.

"Touch yourself," Gabe said.

Her eyes widened briefly, but she did as told, reaching down to touch her clit. Vinny groaned. He remained perfectly quiet, watching, imagining what he'd do to her next.

"I know it's your birthday, but how long you going to keep us waiting?" Archie asked.

"Tonight we're going to triple team her. Proper like."

He knew she couldn't complain. She'd been curious, wondering why they hadn't claimed her together. He'd been cautiously looking forward to this day.

"Hell yeah," Vinny said. "I've never seen a finer ass than hers."

He couldn't believe he wanted to cut her loose in the beginning. After so many failed attempts at a real relationship, he'd given up on love. Annalise made all the difference. Now that they had her, he couldn't imagine life any other way. They were all meant to find each other.

"I'm getting chilly," she said.

"We can't have that, now can we?" Gabe stood up and walked toward her. She looked up at him with those big, green eyes. He used a curled finger to tilt her chin up higher. "So beautiful."

She bit her lip.

"I'm going to fill that virgin ass with my cock tonight, so I want you nice and relaxed. Lie on the sofa and open your legs nice and wide."

Annalise swallowed hard and did as he asked, sitting on the sofa then settling comfortably on her back. Her tits fell slightly to the sides and her knees were still closed tight.

He shook his head. "Let me see my pussy. I bet it's glistening."

She tentatively opened her thighs, her pink swollen pussy on full display for the three of them. They were all around the sofa now—eager and ready.

Vinny leaned over the back of the sofa and pressed two fingers deep into her slick pussy, finger fucking her over and over until she closed her eyes, her rigid body softening.

"That's enough," Gabe said, getting to his knees. He threw one of her legs over his shoulder, shifting her body slightly, then he delved in.

Immediately, she cried out as he lapped up her sensitive folds. He planned to enjoy her, get her loosened up enough for what they had planned. Gabe devoured her cunt, savoring her taste and the way she squirmed against his face.

He noticed Archie bending over to suck her tit deep into his mouth. Within seconds, she detonated, her pussy pulsing on his mouth, her cries filling their farmhouse.

"Get the lube from the first drawer," Gabe said, pointing to the hall console table. Vinny rushed over, grabbing the tube.

"Got it."

"You sure you're ready for this?" Gabe asked her. He brushed her hair off her face. She had a nice flush now, her cheeks a pretty pink.

"I'm ready, but you have too many clothes on."

He'd give her anything she desired. He stood and shrugged off his flannel, tossing it on the chair, then he tugged off his t-shirt, leaving him bare chested. She looked him up and down, her lips parted.

Gabe nodded to Vinny and Archie. He wasn't going to be the only naked man in the room. They all removed their clothes until they were completely bare.

He held out a hand to her, helping her to her feet. She was a bit wobbly, but they were all there to help steady her.

After Archie took her place on the sofa, he

beckoned for her to straddle him.

"Go on, Red, sit on Archie's cock. Tell us how it feels," Vinny said, pumping his own length as he watched her climb over Archie.

She slowly sank down his friend's dick until sitting flush over his groin.

"Tell us," Vinny said.

"I feel so full. He's big and stretching every part of me. I like it, though."

"Of course, you do. You love our cocks, don't you?"

She moaned in response as Archie grabbed her hips and drove up inside of her.

"More," she said.

Gabe didn't waste any time. He took the tube of lube from Vinny and coated his dick from top to bottom, then drizzled a healthy amount down the crack of Annalise's ass. Archie held her down against his chest, her cute little asshole easy to see.

He used one finger and inserted it slowly into her virgin ass. She was tighter than a fist, clenching hard against the intrusion. "You have to relax, baby girl. Relax and push back against me or Vinny'll have to get the ginger root."

She obeyed, always so eager to please.

He added a second finger, scissoring them inside her, stretching her. Gabe wanted her ready and used to being impaled from both sides. Archie was showing considerable restraint, not moving a muscle while he prepared Annalise.

Finally, he mounted her from behind. He got a comfortable enough position with all the legs in the way and poised his erection at her tight rosette.

"Get ready to be double fucked, baby."

****

Vinny's fantasy was coming alive.

He'd been the first to mention a foursome, even getting shit for it, but now it was their reality. His best friends in the world pistoned in and out of Annalise from both ends. It had only taken a few minutes for her to get accustomed to Gabe's big dick up her ass. It was oddly erotic watching the three of them even though he wasn't yet a part of it—but he would be.

He'd made love to Annalise alone and with his friends, but never like this. Vinny palmed his erection a few more times, then walked to the head of the sofa. He grabbed a handful of red hair, tugging her head up. Her eyes were hooded, her lips swollen.

"Suck it, Red. Take it all deep in your throat."

She opened without hesitation, wrapping her beautiful lips around his cock. He closed his eyes and groaned. She bobbed up and down his length, matching the rhythm Gabe and Archie used to fuck her.

It was perfect, all her holes full. They were claiming her as they should. She belonged to them and always would be.

"Come for us, baby. I can't hold off any longer." Gabe gripped her hips, ramming into her ass. One day, Vinny would be in his place, her body stuffed full of so much cock.

"Oh, God," she cried. Annalise returned her attention to his erection, sucking harder. He gritted his teeth, so close to coming down her throat.

"Oh, yeah, that's a girl. Come all over my dick," Archie said.

She pulled off Vinny's cock, gasping and whining until she finally let out a scream that made him come on the spot. He sprayed the sticky white release over her tits as Archie and Gabe finished inside of her. It was filthy. It was perfection.

The next morning, they all sat at the table sipping on their coffees.

"So…" Gabe said.

After such a wild night, things were slightly awkward. He knew Gabe was worried they'd taken things too far and Annalise would be looking for an excuse to get cut loose.

"Are you not hungry?" she asked. "You've hardly touched your eggs."

"Sorry, sweetheart. Just thinking."

"About what?"

There was a wave of silence.

Gabe was never very good at talking or expressing himself, so Vinny cut in. "I think we're all a bit worried about last night."

She frowned, setting down her mug. "What about?"

"It's not exactly like talking about the weather. Did we hurt you? I mean, if you never want to do something like that again, I know we'll all understand," Vinny said.

"Of course," Gabe agreed.

"Is that what all this is about? You're worried I hated last night?"

"Pretty much," Archie said.

She took a bite of her scrambled eggs. "Too bad. I was looking forward to the next time we did it. I don't think I've ever orgasmed so hard."

"You playin'?" Gabe asked.

"I'd never tease you about that. Now why don't the three of you finish your breakfast? There won't be anything else until lunch."

She then continued to eat as if it was any other day. He made discreet eye contact with Gabe and Archie. They looked as pleasantly confused as he was.

He began to feast on his food. Just knowing she wasn't upset made everything right in his world.

After finishing another mouthful, he paused. "You know I didn't mean any of the crude things I said last night. And the hairpulling—"

They'd all gotten real down and dirty last night. It all felt right at the moment, but now he was second-guessing his behavior. He respected Annalise more than any other woman, so he wanted her to understand it was just the lust talking.

"Vinny, it's completely okay. I wouldn't have it any other way." She stood and collected her empty dishes. "I'll hand deliver lunch to the first one of you to finish breakfast. I know how much you all love tractor sex."

Then she walked off.

They had a brief stare-off, and then they all nearly choked down their food.

Their lives weren't ordinary. They didn't match the other families in town or share the same ideals. But they were all hardworking cowboys and strong members of the community. Their private lives were their own business. And they wouldn't change a thing about their foursome. Annalise bonded an already close friendship, cementing it together forever.

For the first time, Vinny looked to the future with hope and optimism. They had their forever woman, and they'd spend the rest of their lives loving her.

The End

SAM CRESCENT AND STACEY ESPINO

www.samcrescent.com

www.staceyespino.com

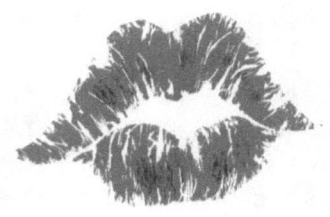

EVERNIGHT PUBLISHING ®

www.evernightpublishing.com

www.ingramcontent.com/pod-product-compliance
Lightning Source LLC
Chambersburg PA
CBHW030616130626
46552CB00002B/599